"Come here," he said, drawing Ali into an embrace.

Burying her face against the smooth, bare skin of his shoulder, she wept for the loss of her library. More than just being unemployed, she didn't know what she was going to do with her life.

Presently the man penetrated her consciousness as something more than a solid shape to comfort her. He smelled good. He felt nice to lean on. His hand smoothing her hair was gentle. Gradually she became aware of all this, aware that the hair on his thighs was prickling the skin on her legs.

That caused different, deeper prickles where no prickles had occurred for a long time. She realized her arms were locked around his firm waist, her fists clenched in the small of his back. She opened them, and that was when she discovered there was no longer the tablecloth between them.

He'd wrapped it around himself as soon as he'd found her crying in the kitchen. Carefully, experimentally, she slid her hand lower, encountering nothing more than skin. Her fingers curved under the shape of him and he drew in a sharp breath.

"Honey," he said. "Don't get me wrong. I like what you're doing just fine, but don't you think we should introduce ourselves first?"

Dear Reader,

Trying to choose one romantic comedy movie as a favorite is an almost impossible task! I don't know if I could narrow down my many, many choices, but that is the question we've been asking our writers as part of our Let's Celebrate sweepstakes. Take a moment to read what our authors have chosen and fill out the entry form to win a collection of romantic comedy videos.

Judy Griffith Gill returns to LOVE & LAUGHTER with *Lady on Top*. Judy made a lot of fans with *There's Something About The Nanny* (LOVE & LAUGHTER #7). *Romantic Times* said, "Judy Griffith Gill's magical storytelling will charm and enthrall readers." Judy continues to delight with her new book, the story of the quiet, prim and proper librarian who decides it's time to add spice to her life!

Colleen Collins has had an interesting and varied career, everything from public relations to working as a personal assistant in Hollywood. Her love for the movies is apparent in her story *Right Chest, Wrong Name*. Have fun, and as you read this dizzying, madcap adventure you will find it really harks back to the great screwball comedies. You can even play talent agent and cast your own movie in your mind!

What's your favorite romantic comedy movie?

With love and laughter,

Malle Vallik

Malle Vallik
Associate Senior Editor

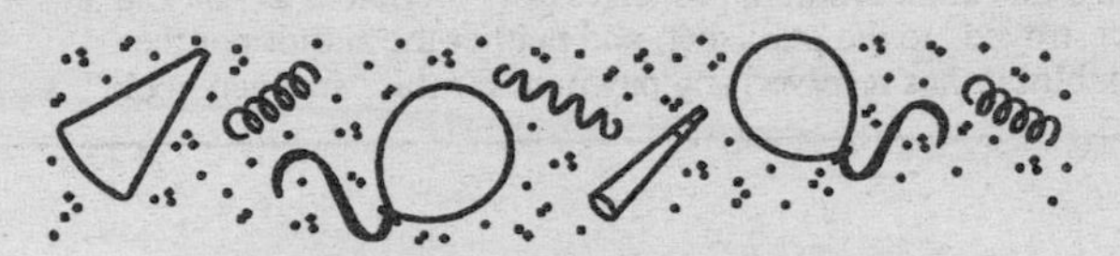

LADY ON TOP

Judy Griffith Gill

Harlequin Books

TORONTO • NEW YORK • LONDON
AMSTERDAM • PARIS • SYDNEY • HAMBURG
STOCKHOLM • ATHENS • TOKYO • MILAN
MADRID • WARSAW • BUDAPEST • AUCKLAND

ISBN 0-373-44025-1

LADY ON TOP

This edition published by arrangement with Harlequin Books S.A.

Printed in U.S.A.

A funny thing happened...

When I write something in a novel, I need to know that it is possible. My heroine, Ali, is flung into the trunk of her own car and it is stolen by a couple of young punks. To take control of the situation, she needs to surprise the thieves. My car has rear seat backs that can be laid forward and flat to carry long loads in the trunk. *Aha!* I thought. *There's Ali's out.* All she needs to do is shove those seat backs forward, roll out into the body of the car and attack the kids with her weapon of choice.

The question was: Is this possible? Reluctantly, but with the kind of determination I wanted Ali to feel, I had my best, most trusted friend lock my claustrophobic self into the trunk of my own car. Wow! Is it dark in there! And close. Along with the claustrophobia, paranoia kicked in, and panic, and horrible thoughts: What if my friend died unexpectedly and no one found either of us for hours? If I had to remain locked in that trunk for more than thirty seconds, I knew I'd go mad.

All these awful emotions worked as a great motivator. I whapped both seat backs out of my way and lunged into the back seat, amazing my (mercifully) perfectly healthy friend with the speed and agility of my escape, thereby proving to my own satisfaction that Ali could just as easily surprise the creeps who had captured her. But I think the thugs were even more surprised when they learned exactly what kind of weapon it was she'd pulled on them....

—Judy Griffith Gill

Books by Judy Griffith Gill

HARLEQUIN LOVE & LAUGHTER

7—THERE'S SOMETHING ABOUT THE NANNY...

With love and gratitude to all of those who
believed in me when I'd stopped believing in myself.
You know who you are.

1

ALI KOZINSKI'S FIRST GLIMMER of self-dissatisfaction began one July Saturday night at 10:25, with a call from her cousin Cindy Saunders.

"Hi, Ali. Is my watch wrong?" Cindy said apologetically. "I thought I'd catch you before you got ready for bed, but it sounds like you have a mouthful of toothpaste."

Ali did. Feeling mildly annoyed, she spit it out. Was she really *so* predictable that everyone in the family knew she went to bed at ten-thirty every night? Including Saturday?

"Not at all," she said. "I had a mouthful of whipping cream I just licked off the guy who posed for Mr. July on the Firemen Hunks calendar."

Cindy laughed indulgently. "Yeah, right."

Ali dragged the phone cord with her as she went back to her bedroom where there was, naturally, no hunk and no whipping cream. Though Mr. July did look down from his page above Ali's desk. "Sounds as if *you're* at a party."

Of course, everyone in the family also could have predicted that Cindy would be partying on a Saturday night, so maybe there was no difference.

"About our tennis date tomorrow morning,"

Cindy said. "I have to beg off. I won't be back in time. I've been asked to go sailing and the guys are leaving right now. I haven't been sailing in *ages*. And there's *such* a moon! I'll call you Monday, okay?"

While Cindy went sailing off in the moonlight with men, Ali crawled into bed *alone*, yanking the covers over her head.

She rose at six-thirty, because that was the time she always got up.

Sundays included.

After tidying the kitchen, she shoved her feet into gardening shoes and went out to weed the three long rows of carrots next to the fence. It was their turn.

"Alison... Oh, Al-i-son!" Her next-door neighbor's call brought Ali to her feet. "Good morning, Mrs. Rathbury."

"Ah, I knew you'd be at the carrots today." Short little Mrs. Rathbury, obviously standing on something to get high enough, clung to the top of the fence and peered over at Ali and the half-weeded carrot rows. "You did the tomatoes yesterday."

"Yes." Alison glanced at the staked tomato plants and the plump, still green fruit hanging over freshly worked soil around their roots. *Damn!* It was becoming clearer and clearer. She was so predictable even her neighbor had her schedule down pat, including *when* she was going to weed *what*.

"I have a favor to ask, dear. I wasn't scheduled

for Altar Guild this week, but one of my friends who was, fell down the stairs this morning and was rushed to hospital. I've been asked to fill in for her. But my young great-nephew Joey is visiting. I don't want to disturb him and tell him I need to go out—the poor boy's exhausted—but nor do I want him waking up all alone in a strange house. Would you be good enough to come over and stay until he gets up? Maybe you could make him a bite of breakfast, too?''

Ali smiled and nodded. ''Sure, Mrs. Rathbury. I'd be happy to baby-sit your great-nephew. How old—''

A car's horn honked out on the street and Mrs. Rathbury, with a quick wave, hopped off whatever she was standing on, and rushed up the flagged walkway past her house, disappearing behind a hedge.

Ali rinsed her hands under the outdoor faucet, snatched the Sunday paper off the porch and went quickly through the side gate to Mrs. Rathbury's before the little nephew woke up.

Inside her neighbor's familiar kitchen, the coffee on the stove sent its aromatic ''drink me'' message and, though she'd had her normal two-cup ration, Ali complied.

There, she thought with some satisfaction. *I'm breaking out already.* Three cups of coffee was certainly a change in routine.

The main newspaper headline reached up and slapped her in the face. In the big, bold, stop-the-presses kind of type usually reserved for declarations of war, it read: Library Burns Overnight.

The library? *Her* library? No! Impossible! It had been fine when she left the previous day at six p.m. after locking up. Maybe they meant some other library?

Ali forced herself to focus on the text of the article.

"The alarm was turned in at 11:04 last night, but by the time firefighters arrived three minutes later, the building was fully involved."

"No," she moaned softly. "No! Oh, no! It can't be!"

But clearly it could, it was. "Arson is suspected," she read, then reared back. *Arson?*

A sudden and irrational mental image of the mayor gleefully holding a lighted match to a pile of books came to mind. He was on record as wanting the Mitikiltuk library to join forces with the one in Kentonville as a cost-cutting measure. So far, only a minority of council had come on side with him.

Ali groaned. Her breastbone ached. Her teeth hurt. Her skin burned. Was she having a heart attack?

Stumbling to her feet, she clenched her fists.

She choked, tried to set down her coffee cup, but could only grip it tightly, watching it shake uncontrollably in her hand.

Unaccustomed fiery emotion erupted in her chest, filling her every pore, pumping adrenaline through nerve and muscle making her feel as if she was going to explode. This very second!

"No!" she yelled as one of Mrs. Rathbury's precious Royal Albert *Blossom Time* cups flew from her hand. *"No!"*

The cup smashed against the wall, shattered, leaving a brown shape streaming down cheerful yellow paint.

KEITH WAS ON HIS FEET before he was awake.

"No!"

The anguished howl set him in motion. He flung himself from his bedroom as it came again. "No!"

He raced along the corridor and lunged through the kitchen doorway. He screeched to an abrupt halt. Clutching the door frame, he stared in astonishment at the woman who stood with her back to him, shattered pieces of china sprinkling the floor at her feet.

"Take *that,* Mr. Mayor!" she said as she drew back her arm and the saucer followed the cup. It smashed in the middle of the wall between the plate-shaped clock with spoons for hands, and a calendar from Victoria's Butchart Gardens. The woman then grabbed the sugar bowl and flung it, sending a glittering cascade of crystals showering across the kitchen. It ricocheted harmlessly off one of those ugly, shrunken-faced cloth dolls his aunt had hanging all over the house, and landed safely in a basket of laundry.

She'd have flung the cream pitcher, but for Keith's shout.

"Hold it!"

With the pitcher dangling loosely, she whirled to stare at him, her blue eyes wide, her pink lips parted. Wisps of blond hair had escaped from what looked like a bun wound so tight she'd never grow a wrinkle. Her mouth gaped open. Following the direction of her shocked gaze, he snatched the cloth off the table, sending a newspaper, a spoon and a duck-shaped holder full of paper napkins flying. He wrapped the tablecloth around his waist.

"What the hell are you doing?" he demanded. So much for quiet. So much for no screams in the night! The sunshine told him it was no longer night, but he'd still been asleep so the principle was the same.

She took a step back as he tucked in the ends of the tablecloth. "Who are you?" he snapped. "What the hell is going on?"

She said nothing. He watched her throat work. Color came, went, came, went, and then stayed out of her face. "What happened here?" he asked, her stricken expression softening his tone. Clearly, bellowing at a crazed woman wasn't the way to go.

"I...I broke a cup." She crouched and began gathering up the scattered shards, looping the handle over her pinkie. "And a saucer."

"So I see." Her face looked as if it were about to shatter as the china had, and her hands shook so hard the bits she'd collected rattled together. One of them cut her. Blood oozed out, and dripped from her palm to her knee. She seemed oblivious.

Spilled sugar gritty under his bare feet, Keith approached carefully, skirting the pink and white bits of broken china. He wrapped one hand around her wrist and drew her to her feet. He picked the pieces off her hand, set them on the table and led her past the rest of the sharp shards on the floor. At the sink, he turned on the cold water and rinsed the blood off her palm.

After checking the small cut at the base of her fingers, he pressed his thumb over it to stem the bleeding, all the while keeping a wary eye on her in case she blew up again.

Ali stared at her pink palm cradled on the man's large, brown hand, the broad, clean nail, the hard pad of his thumb applying pressure. She tried to think of something sensible to say, assuming she could ever unlock her throat. Her anger spent, she felt weak, exhausted. She'd have liked nothing more than to skulk off somewhere and hide from what she'd done.

"Does breakin[illegible] up always make you scream at the mayor?" [illegible]ad a kind voice, and as he gazed at her wit[illegible] expression of baffled sympathy, she became self-conscious. In comparison with his dark brown hair and swarthy tan, her blond hair and fair skin seemed washed out.

Ali shook her head. "The books. The books are all gone," she said in a raspy voice.

"I see."

She blinked her eyes against the unexpected burn of tears and lifted her free hand to clamp it over her mouth. But nothing could stem her desperate urge to weep.

"Ah, hey, now. Come on, come here," he said, drawing her into an embrace. Burying her face against the smooth, bare skin of his shoulder, she wept for the loss of her library, only half aware of the warm hand between her shoulder blades, rubbing, rubbing, rubbing.

Presently the man penetrated her consciousness as something more than a solid shape to comfort her. He smelled good. He felt nice to lean on. His arms were muscular, hard as they crossed her back, but his hand smoothing her hair, massaging her scalp, was gentle. Gradually she became aware of all this, then aware that the hair on his thighs was prickling the skin on her legs.

That caused different, deeper prickles where no prickles had occurred for a long time. She moved restlessly in his embrace, sliding her cheek across the slick, tear-wet skin of his shoulder. She realized her arms were locked around his firm waist, her fists clenched in the small of his back. She opened them, and that was when she discovered there was no tablecloth between them and his flesh.

Tablecloth? Egads!

Had he dropped it, or had it just slid down a couple of inches? Carefully, experimentally, she slid her hands lower, encountering nothimg more than skin. Her fingers curved under the shape of him and he drew in a sharp breath.

"Honey," he said. "Don't get me wrong. I like what you're doing just fine, but don't you think we should introduce ourselves first?"

Ali emitted a hoarse little squawk and leaped back.

For what seemed like endless moments, she stood staring at the tousled, unshaven man who stared back at her, his dark eyebrows drawn together, one fist clutching the bunched tablecloth in front of him.

At least six feet tall, he had broad shoulders, muscular arms, a hairy chest and wore only that tablecloth. It was a small one. Pale pink. With embroidered magenta pansies on its four corners. As she watched, he carefully, discreetly, wrapped the cloth around him again, drawing two sets of pansies one over the other and tucking them in. The other two sets hung loose at the side of his left thigh. He breathed in, and the two tucked sets threatened to separate.

He returned her stare. She didn't suppose he'd like for a minute what he saw. Her face always swelled up and her eyes got as pink as a rabbit's when she cried, and to top it off, she was blushing.

Thoroughly embarrassed by her appearance and her outburst, Ali whirled away from him, stumbled into a chair and sank onto it, burying her face in her arms on the table.

"Come on, honey, take it easy," he said, rubbing her back again. He sounded impatient. She felt the bare skin of his stomach against her arm and shivered.

"Try to calm down and tell me who you are so I can call someone to come and get you." Obviously he thought she was weeping again. Just as obviously he thought she was a lunatic who needed to be humored.

She didn't lift her head. *Couldn't.*

"I don't need someone to take me home." To her dismay, she actually was weeping again. Because of his kindness. It undid her. "I just need my...books...back." It came out in great, gulping, childish sobs.

"Oh, yes. Your books. Where do you suppose they went?" he asked.

"Up there." With a wave of one hand, she indicated the stratosphere. "In little wisps of smo-o-oke, bits of ashes."

His back rub continued. Ridiculously her crying did, too. She seemed incapable of stopping it. "Fahrenheit f-f-four fifty-one," she sobbed.

"What's that?"

"A book," she said, looking up in surprise, forgetting all about her red face, rabbit eyes and puffy cheeks. Didn't everyone know that book? "By Ray Bradbury. A cla-a-assic."

She accepted the handful of paper napkins he offered her, and wiped her face. "And now it's gone." A quick peek told her his tablecloth, at least, was not gone. It was securely tucked around his body. For the moment. If only he'd quit breathing, moving.

She stared so long at the folded pink fabric against his waist that she stopped crying.

"You said books. Plural."

She jerked her gaze back in the general direction of his face. "Yes. Thousands!"

"All by this Bradbury guy?"

"No, of course not. I mean, he was prolific, but no one author writes 'thousands' of books. I guess I thought of that title because four hundred fifty-one degrees Fahrenheit is the temperature at which paper burns. At which that book, all my b-books burned."

She nearly choked up again, but after a moment with her face hidden in the napkins, she bent, retrieved the newspaper from the floor and shoved it at him.

He sat in a chair at right angles to her, head tilted, a question in his eyes, looking not at the paper, but at her. She watched in horrified fascination as he crossed an ankle over a knee. The tablecloth held, creating strategic shadows. She breathed again.

"The library," she said, tapping the coffee-stained front page picture. "There was a fire last night. I work there. *Worked* there, but now—" She broke off, unwilling to voice the question, *What am I going to do now?* The library was her life!

Taking refuge in action, Ali jumped to her feet, grabbed a broom from the closet next to the fridge and swept up the remaining bits of china. What in the world was she going to say to Mrs. Rathbury? She cringed. She'd have to tell the truth, of course, as unlikely as she knew her neighbor would find it, and she'd go out first thing Monday to replace the broken items.

She wiped down the yellow-painted wall, glad to see the coffee hadn't left a stain, then mopped up the floor.

Keith, recalling the trucks and hoses downtown last night, scanned the article, frowning as he read interviews with the fire chief, the mayor and the director of the library governing board.

They speculated on the value of the loss—in the millions; discussed insurance coverage—insufficient; and considered the chances of a new library replacing the old one anytime soon—next to nil.

The director lamented the four jobs, but was quick to point out that the Kentonville library was more than able to take up the slack. He agreed that, yes, it might be an inconvenience for the populace to travel thirty miles to Kentonville. But it was, he pointed out, a much newer facility, and large enough to adequately serve the whole area.

The mayor was quoted as saying it was a tragedy, but funding was so short he couldn't foresee a quick solution to the problem of no library in town. "The loss of this wonderful old heritage building is more devastating to me than the loss of the books."

Keith glanced up at the woman industriously

cleaning up the mess she'd made. He supposed she was one of those who had lost her job overnight. No wonder she was upset with the mayor who didn't seem at all disposed to finding the funds for rebuilding.

As if sensing his stare, she turned, a guilty expression on her face. "Oh, Lord," she said. "I'm supposed to be making you breakfast, too. I will, as soon as I finish up here. I'm sorry. You must be starved."

"Breakfast?" He stood and as her eyes widened in apprehension, belatedly made sure his cloth was securely wrapped. Her nervousness amused him, tempted him to drop his covering just to see her blush. Blushing enhanced the blue of her eyes.

With her hair loose like that, she was more than just passably pretty. Under all those freckles, she had the kind of bone structure that would wear well, and her body—now there was a shape that begged a man to trace it with his hands and— *Hold it, Devon, you're not in the market for fun and games!*

The thought startled him. *I'm not?*

No. Not with this kind of woman.

2

ALI WATCHED different emotions play across the man's face. "Why would you want to make me breakfast?" he said, his eyes narrowing.

"Because I promised I would," she said.

She rinsed her hands and dried them before bending to find a frying pan in the drawer under Mrs. Rathbury's stove. She set it on a burner, turned it on to medium then opened the refrigerator.

"Hold it!" His long arm reached out, grabbed the bacon package and slapped it back down onto the wire shelf, making the salad dressing bottles rattle.

He shut the refrigerator with a solid thud. His fingers clamped over the points of Ali's shoulders, holding her in place. His brown eyes were no longer soft.

"Let's get down to a few basics here. To begin with, who are you, what are you doing in this house, and what have you done with my aunt?"

Ali gasped. "What have I done with— Well, for heaven's sake! Nothing! What do you think I am, some kind of secret ax-murder who does in old ladies so I can cook breakfast in their kitchens?"

"Could be."

"Well, I'm not. I'm Ali Kozinski. I'm...I'm your, uh, the—"

Suddenly she realized how ludicrous this entire situation was. What had Mrs. Rathbury been thinking of? She knew her neighbor was getting on in years, but she certainly wasn't senile, so why did she think her nephew needed a...a... "Baby-sitter," she said aloud with as much authority as she could muster.

He laughed in what she took to be relief. "You're in the wrong house. This is Ruth Rathbury's place. I'm Keith Devon, her nephew, and we do not need a baby-sitter. I don't have any babies to be sat."

"I'm not supposed to be looking after *your* babies. I'm supposed to be looking after Mrs. Rathbury's great-nephew. What are you doing here?"

He dropped his hands from her shoulders, took one step back and the lower two clusters of pansies parted company again to expose a great deal of skin. Ali stared, holding her breath as the upper two began to slip apart, too. He hitched the tablecloth back together. Her gaze followed its tight line across his flat belly, down the inverted V-shaped opening that revealed a lot of hard, brown thigh.

She frowned at that thigh. "Are you Joey's father? Doesn't Mrs. Rathbury think you're capable of looking after him?"

Actually was he capable? Running around in the altogether...well, it said something, didn't it?

"Joey?" he echoed, and she forced her gaze upward, then turned the heat off under the pan.

"I haven't been called that in thirty years," he went on. "The old lady's losing it."

"You're Joey?"

"Apparently." He let go of his cloth and rammed one hand through his hair, laughing, but his words evidenced his exasperation. "Cripes! I've been taking care of myself forever. Why the hell did she think I'd need a baby-sitter?"

Ali thought back. "Maybe she didn't say that, not exactly. I guess I made a wrong assumption. She said she had to go out, and that you were sleeping, you were exhausted. She referred to you as a 'poor boy,' and said she didn't want you waking up alone in a strange house, and asked me to come over and stay here until you were awake. And to cook your breakfast."

He put his hands on his narrow hips and smiled at her, his lids still half covering his eyes, so she couldn't tell if it was a friendly smile or a menacing one. For some reason not knowing increased her heart rate alarmingly. Oddly, instead of making her feel timid, as if she should run away, his enigmatic smile induced a totally unfamiliar sensation of adventurousness, boldness, daring. A ridiculous vision rose in her mind of whipped cream slowly sliding down his chest.

"And after letting her bulldoze you into it," he said, "you threw a tantrum the minute she was gone?"

His question wiped away all thoughts of whipped cream.

"I did not throw a tantrum," Ali replied stiffly, aghast as well as offended.

He laughed. "Lady, that's sure what it looked like from where I stood."

"That's ridiculous. I never throw tantrums! I'm well-known for being...placid."

He laughed again. He actually laughed at her, loudly and rudely. Mercifully those big hands splayed on his hipbones over the top edge of the tablecloth held it in place. "I could think of several descriptives, but that wouldn't be among them." He grinned. "If you don't throw tantrums, you at least throw dishes. Shows a certain...shall we say...spirit?"

Was that admiration in his tone? The notion startled her. It also pleased her. She didn't think anyone at all, let alone a man, had ever considered her "spirited."

"Say whatever you like." Ali tilted her chin. "My emotional outburst had nothing to do with your aunt's request that I look after Joe—er, you. If I hadn't wanted to agree to her request, I would have said no."

She stared at one small curl of hair on his chest. It was exactly the same size as the tip of her pinkie. She curled her fingers into fists and stuffed them behind her back, to keep her pinkie out of trouble.

"But you obviously don't need a baby-sitter, and

since your waking up alone in a strange house is no longer an issue, I'll go back to my weeding."

Grateful for the excuse to escape before he lost his cloth or she lost her mind waiting for it to happen, she turned and made for the back door.

"Hold it!"

It seemed to be his favorite phrase, and one that worked. She froze in place. For the second time, one of his long arms whipped out and his fingers wrapped around her wrist, whirling her back to face him as if they were on a dance floor.

Ali stumbled, caught her breath and held it as she came up hard against his chest. If someone had tried to drive a straw between them, there'd have been no room, but could she move? Did she want to move?

Yes. Closer. Only closer.

Again, the impact of Ali Kozinski's firm, lithe body against his rocked Keith. He liked it. After a moment, when she stopped standing stiffly, staring up at him with apprehension, he realized she, too, liked it. He enjoyed the blush rising up her throat, over her face until even her scalp turned pink at the roots of her pale gold hair.

Her bemused expression, a delightful blend of shock, fear, pleasure and wonder made him smile. Tentatively she smiled back and he toyed with the intriguing idea of kissing her. She drew in a tremulous breath, and let it sigh out.

He couldn't resist. He bent his head and brushed his mouth over hers, once, quickly, but even that was too much—along with being not nearly enough. The feel of her lips, velvety smooth, the scent of her skin, warm and womanly, the sound of her soft rapid breathing nearly tumbled him headfirst into a situation he neither needed nor wanted.

But he wanted just one more tiny taste. He took it, felt her lips tremble, part, and experienced the joy of watching her gilt eyelashes flutter shut. He brushed the pad of his thumb over her lips, bent, replaced it with his mouth and then, quickly, while he still could, he released her.

Maintaining only a light grasp on her wrist, he felt her pulse hammering as rapidly as his own. Somehow, he managed what he hoped was a casual grin, one that hid his too-potent response to her.

"Now I know *I'm* in the right house, and *you're* in the right house, having someone cook me breakfast sounds like a great idea."

"But I—" Her eyes dropped to the scant covering, then swept back to his face. He forced himself to stifle his laughter. Shy and uncertain, she stood there terrified he might drop his loincloth at any second.

Hell! With the kind of luck he'd been having lately, she'd turn out to be a nun in civvies. Still, some devil in him tempted him to let the tablecloth slip again just to see her reaction.

Nah. It wouldn't be fair. Fun, yes, but not fair. He caught the top edges in a fist as she added, "And you—"

"Need to get dressed. I know," he interrupted smoothly. "And I will, as soon as you promise to stay and have breakfast with me."

"I've already had breakfast." She flicked her gaze toward the wall clock. "It's after eight-thirty."

By God, she sounded more than just mildly scandalized. "Is 'after eight-thirty' such a terrible time to be considering Sunday breakfast?" As far as he was concerned, it was an indecently early hour for a man on vacation. If she hadn't started trashing his aunt's kitchen, he'd still be sacked out in a nice, comfortable bed, soothed by the sound of the lake lapping at the shore. Instead, here he stood in the kitchen, anything but soothed.

"Not at all," she said, sounding huffy and insulted. "It's just not part of my routine."

He cocked his head to one side. "Routine?"

"Of course. Don't you have one?"

He laughed. "Not noticeably. I've never found one necessary."

But he had planned to establish a routine during this very necessary vacation. And that was going to run something like early to bed, late to rise, and no alarms in the night.

Then, came Ali, throwing tantrums, cups and saucers—and him for a loop. He had to smile.

He tugged gently, wanting her up against his chest, thinking how it would feel to cover her half-parted lips with his own again and this time—

Ali jerked her hand free, took a step back from

him, and crossed her arms in front of herself. Whether it was a result of the earlier, nagging feeling that she was becoming too set in her ways, or because of the hint of challenge she heard in his tone, saw in his eyes, she lifted her chin and met his amused gaze.

For reasons she would never understand, instead of merely walking out the door, she prolonged their encounter.

"All right. I'll cook your breakfast since everyone has to keep body and soul together." In actual fact, she was more concerned about him keeping body and tablecloth together.

"I'll do it. You sit down and be my guest. Entertain me."

He leaned past her and turned on the heat under the frying pan again before opening the fridge. "How many slices?"

She stepped back. "I told you. I already had breakfast."

"Oh, come on," he said, catching that damned, suicidal tablecloth of his again as the pansies made a dive for the floor. "Live dangerously."

She wished for the courage to tell him he and his scant covering were enough danger for her for one morning. For one lifetime! Her heart rollicked around in her chest, so lively it felt as if it would escape any second.

"I'd enjoy having breakfast with a pretty woman." He slid an extremely blatant and gratifyingly appreciative stare over her and her gardening clothes.

Pretty? He thought she was pretty? Pretty *and* spirited? Didn't she wish! But that was not Ali. It might have been Cindy, but certainly not Ali. And men never found her entertaining.

She was wearing a skimpy pair of shorts she'd had since she was thirteen, and a tank top of similar vintage. After twenty years of launderings, both garments were ready for the ragbag, but garden soil couldn't hurt them and they were comfortable.

She, however, was not comfortable with the way he looked at her. Nor was she comfortable with her response when he touched her. All he did was use one finger to lift a wisp of hair away from the corner of her mouth. He slid it across her cheek, tucking the hair behind her ear. A deep, sensual shudder shook her. But at least her heart stopped flopping around like crazy.

It stopped, period.

She shook her head, dislodging his finger. How had it come undone? He must have pulled out her pins when she was crying and stroking her hair. Dammit, that was why she kept her hair confined to a bun. It was much too uncontrollable to be allowed to have its head.

She had to bite back a giggle as the unintended pun caused her to do a mental double-take, but she couldn't prevent a smile.

"What's the joke?" he asked, and when she shook her head, still fighting that bubbling sensation in her chest, he touched the fullness of her bottom lip with that same fingertip. "Come on. Share."

"No." Dammit, she was thirty-three years old. She did not giggle.

And men did not look at her the way this one was looking.

Oh, what was she thinking? A man like him probably *practiced* that look on every woman he met. Yet, as he continued to gaze at her, he managed despite her discomfort, despite her doubts, to make her feel special. Under the faintly questioning stare from those brown eyes, she began to feel as if she could be the first woman he'd ever really looked at in his life.

As if she was, as he'd said, "a pretty woman," instead of just plain old Alison Kozinski who had freckles and a life sentence of bad-hair days.

It made her heart beat faster, made it difficult to inhale and told her she'd be wise to run. He was just another summer visitor.

Leo had been a summer visitor initially, too.

She thought, over the years, she'd met all of Mrs. Rathbury's large family, but it seemed she hadn't.

If he came to visit his great aunt so infrequently, it wasn't likely he'd be back again anytime soon.

Not that she wanted him to be, of course. He was the same kind of person, one with no routine, one who didn't even think such a thing was necessary, as her mother and stepfather, her peripatetic brothers, as her husband had been. She'd been cursed by being born to a family of nomads.

That lack of clear direction, lack of stability, had really bothered her when she'd been growing up, and made her even more unhappy with Leo, so she certainly didn't want another man of the same ilk disturbing her schedule.

What schedule? an inner voice asked. *You're out of a job, Ali. So what are you going to do to keep busy?*

She'd just begun to ponder the vast emptiness of her life when Keith said, "Besides, it wouldn't hurt you to have two breakfasts in one day. You look like you might have had a cup of yogurt and half a grapefruit for the first one."

"How could you possib—" She broke off, wishing she'd kept her mouth shut.

Again, he laughed.

Ali felt heat flood her face. Somehow, his zeroing in with such deadly accuracy infuriated her, but not so much as her inadvertently letting him know he'd guessed right. Predictable! That was her! Even a total stranger could figure her out in half a second. Whatever happened to feminine mystique? Was she utterly lacking in it? Maybe it was time she changed that, too.

Changed? How? Changed what? The only thing in her life that was different was being out of a job.

A moment's swift reflection produced the notion that maybe unemployment *wasn't* so bad. Wouldn't it amaze all the people who thought she was so reliable, so set in her ways, so...predictable, if she simply up and left town?

What would a "pretty, spirited" woman do if she ran away from home to prove a point? Join Hell's Angels?

She laughed aloud, thinking of herself astride a Harley, black helmet covering her bun, librarian's skirt hitched up over her thighs, the wind whipping her face...

"Now what's funny?" Keith asked, jolting her back to reality. "If you're going to stand there smirking and snickering and not telling me what it's all about, you'll convince me I'm the butt of your joke, and destroy my ego."

Ali laughed again. "I have a feeling your ego can stand up to a lot of battering."

"I don't think so," he said, eyes going suddenly serious. "Not from you."

As she met his gaze, that curious sense of excitement or fear or anticipation swept over her again, and Ali sidled away from him. What she should do is leave that instant, get in her car, drive to the nearest airport and hop a flight to...to Ecuador.

Ecuador? Where in the world had that come from? Oh. Right. Yesterday she'd tacked up a poster for Ecuador and the Galápagos Islands on the wall near the travel section in the library. It, too, would be gone.

But, she reasoned, the real thing wouldn't be...

"Now," he cajoled, breaking into her thoughts

again, "didn't you promise my aunt you'd look after me?"

Well, yes, she had.

"You strike me as a lady who keeps promises."

Well, yes, she was that, too.

He continued to watch her face, *reading* her, she knew, recognizing her hesitation, and as a result of it, slapping about three times too many slices of bacon all higgledy-piggledy into the too-hot pan.

He thought she was staying.

She was about to tell him again she was not, when he began shaking the sizzling, smoking pan so vigorously she could only hold her breath and stare in horror at the white strip of flesh curving into the tan of his lower back. The ever-widening pale strip of flesh that suddenly became a complete, bare, pearly-white male backside that showed how brief his swim trunks must be. The pansies planted themselves on the floor.

All he said was, "Oops."

Ali squeezed her eyes shut, bit her lip, and when he called "Coast's clear," from the hallway, she opened them a slit to see a set of purple pansies flitting around the corner and out of sight.

"Go home, Ali," she said sternly. "Go home *now.*"

But instead, she turned down the heat under the pan and tried to turn down the heat burning through herself. Breathing deeply, slowly, she deliberately selected a fork from one of Mrs. Rathbury's tidy kitchen drawers and began straightening out the mishmash of bacon strips.

Clearly the man was *not* capable of cooking breakfast for himself.

And just as clearly, Ali Kozinski needed her head examined.

"WHAT THE HELL is the matter with your head?" Keith muttered to himself as he shaved. He twisted his mouth sideways to get the whiskers on one side of his jaw.

He was smart enough to see when he'd been set up, and this was damn well one of those times. It wasn't the first occasion when his family had brought in a "friend" for him to meet during his vacation, and it probably wouldn't be the last.

But he wasn't looking for a woman, despite what he might have thought about Ali Kozinski a few minutes ago. That hadn't been his *head* working at all.

Now that he was out of her strangely captivating presence, he could recognize that. He had no business even looking at her kind of woman.

So what if she'd felt good in his arms? He'd fit better physically with other women, taller women, and let's face it, Ali Kozinski had to be a good six inches shorter than he, and a hundred pounds lighter.

He dried his face and neck briskly with a towel. What worried him now was the eerie sensation they'd fit together in other ways. More important ways than the mere physical. Nonsexual ways. She looked like someone who could use a friend.

She also looked like someone who could be a friend.

It was a long time since any woman had provided more than just temporary release for him, had offered him more. But then, he hadn't been looking, and if it had been offered, he'd have bugged out. Fast.

As he should right now. Yup. Absolutely. He tugged on his jeans.

He knew he should go out there and tell her he was aware of why she was in his aunt's house. He shoved his arms into the sleeves of a gray T-shirt and pulled it over his head. He should explain he was there for nothing more than a rest, a respite from guns and bombs and shrieks in the night. He wasn't looking for any kind of relationship, but especially not one with a shy, blushing librarian, despite her unexpectedly volatile temper.

A volatile temper that hinted at other, potential passions he'd like to explore and...

No! Because that woman out there in his aunt's kitchen was not territory to be "explored" before moving on to the next one.

That woman was a forever kind, the kind who'd be looking for a man to stay home and cut the grass on Sunday, take the kids to the park and read them bedtime stories. He tucked in the T-shirt and zipped his jeans.

He was not that man despite what his brother tried to convince him.

"You're getting too old to dodge," Dan had said last week. "It's time to stop risking your life for pictures of dead bodies. Where's the glamour in that?"

Keith shrugged. "Where's the glamour in managing a truck stop?"

"Who said I was looking for glamour? That's your department."

But Keith knew of late he, too, had been seeing less of the glamorous gloss he liked to think his life had, and more of the grit. He'd admitted as much to Dan. And admitted, too, he'd been scared more often than usual this past year, and liked it less, hence his need for a spell of total quiet. No guts, no glory? Was he running out of guts? Could he live without the glory?

"I'd say you need more than 'a spell' of it," Dan had continued.

"Yeah? Like what? Settling down and writing a daily column on urban affairs?"

"Write what you want, but yeah, I think settling down's a good idea." That was when Dan, as had his parents, suggested Keith come up here to Aunt Ruth's.

Under the circumstances, it seemed suddenly suspicious that now, in Aunt Ruth's kitchen, there stood a woman who looked as if she might make it worthwhile putting "someday" a lot closer to the top of his list. Obviously his family all knew who lived next door to Ruth, and knew, too, the old lady's propensity for matchmaking.

They were all in cahoots.

Well, he had news for his parents, his brother, his aunt and, since she was undoubtedly part of this conspiracy, Ali Kozinski. "Someday" in Keith's books was a good ten years away from whatever age he happened to be at any given time.

Which was, he decided, exactly what he was going to tell her. He sniffed the aroma of bacon, and grinned.

He'd tell her, sure. Right after breakfast. After all, a man had to eat. He couldn't ignore *all* his appetites.

3

KEITH'S JEANS, Ali discovered when he returned, hair damp from the shower, weren't much of an improvement over the tablecloth. They clung tightly to his form, faded in...interesting spots. She jerked her gaze upward and discovered his T-shirt wasn't a vast improvement over his bare skin, either. It showed every muscle. Really, did the man have to be so blatantly male?

He'd shaved, and as he walked by, a whiff of his soap mingled with the scent of bacon. He stood too close to her as he took a wire whisk from a floral-patterned jug of kitchen implements on the counter and began to beat the eggs she'd cracked into a bowl.

He gave her a sidelong glance, from her head to her feet, then back upward until his gaze rested on her hips, then her breasts for several seconds too long. He cracked two more eggs into the bowl and whipped them harder.

For heaven's sake! Did he think she needed fattening up? Did he find her shape so lacking?

His elbow brushed hers as she buttered toast and he stirred the eggs solidifying golden in the pan.

Ali glanced at him. "Have you...have you ever been to the Galápagos Islands?"

He looked at her in startled astonishment. "Well, um, no. Lots of other places, but not there. I don't think they've held a war or an insurrection during my lifetime. Why?"

War or insurrection? Instead of asking, Ali lifted her chin and met his quizzical gaze. "Because now I have no job, I plan to go there. Next week."

As she said it, she felt strength building within her. Determination. Resolution. She, Ali Kozinski, librarian, steady, reliable, *predictable,* was about to change.

BEFORE SHE REALIZED IT, Ali had eaten three slices of bacon, two pieces of toast, more scrambled eggs than she thought had been her share, but since he'd doled them out, she'd had little choice. And she'd enjoyed every bite.

She'd also had two more cups of coffee. It must have been the overdose of caffeine humming so vigorously through her nervous system that made her talk the way she did.

They weren't even halfway through breakfast when she'd told Keith Devon more about herself than she'd ever told another person on so short an acquaintance. Or, come to think of it, on long acquaintance.

She'd led a particularly boring life and, as Leo had so often told her, no one was interested in that; no one was interested in her. He'd have done better, he'd informed her on more than one occasion, to have married her cousin Cindy. She, at least, would have known how to impress the businessmen he was trying to court with his ideas and propositions.

Ali wasn't stupid and she was a quick learner; she knew she wasn't very interesting. She found it better to turn the conversation away from herself and back to the other person's activities and interests.

Yet, something in Keith Devon's eyes kept her talking about herself. He brushed aside her remarks about her vivacious cousin, and looked genuinely interested when she talked about her own life. He asked questions in a quiet, unobtrusive way, then gave her lots of time to answer. In fact, he would sit so silently, so attentively waiting, she found herself digging deeper into her store of memories so she could tell him a little more, and a little more, and a little more. She started with one incident in her childhood and it flowed from there.

And he showed every sign of wanting her to.

No other man of her acquaintance had ever encouraged her to talk about herself. Usually men said something like, "Now, tell me all about yourself. How do *you* like my car?"

Keith listened intently as she spoke of her father's death—she didn't remember him—her mother's remarriage a year later, and the four brothers who had appeared in quick succession.

"We moved a lot," she said.

"That made you sad," he commented. "Why?"

Ali had to consider that before she said, "I'm not exactly sure." She smiled, then shrugged. "I guess I wanted a place I could count on, Christmas in the same house two years running, a school where I wasn't the perennial new girl. I wanted the kind of life my cousins had right here in Mitikiltuk." She laughed. "The kind of life Cindy hated."

"Since you've come here," he said, smoothing his fingertips over her balled-up fists, making them relax while the rest of her body tensed hummingtaut at his touch, "have you found the life you've always wanted?"

"Yes. Yes, I have." She glanced out the window at the weeping willows on the shore, the glimpses of blue water visible through their feathery branches. "I live next door in what was my grandmother's house. She left it to me. I've always been grateful for that. It represents security to me."

"When did you come? I used to visit Aunt Ruth with my family till I was in my midteens, but I don't remember ever seeing you."

"I spent some vacations with my grandmother—my biological father's mother—but very few. Often, we were too far away for me to make the trip, which was sad, because I know she wanted more of my time. She always said I was just like my dad, quiet, serene, as unruffled as the lake on a June morning."

He smiled. "I've seen that lake kicking up quite a storm on occasion."

Ali bit her lip. As he'd seen her kicking up a storm. That he was the only one to have ever witnessed such an event seemed, oddly, to be all right, to bring them closer together, as if they shared a secret, might share many more.

She jerked her mind out of that groove. She might be looking for change, but not that much of a change. This man was not for her—assuming, of course, she needed a man in any way, shape or form, or for any reason. Which she did not.

"I'd just finished college when Grandma had a stroke and couldn't be left alone. I came to live with her and I've been here ever since except for—" She let it go by jumping up to put on another pot of coffee, since they'd used up all Mrs. Rathbury had left. Mrs. Rathbury sipped on coffee all day long.

"Except for what?" he asked as she filled the pot with water.

"I was married. It didn't...last."

"I'm sorry."

She shrugged, wiped the counter then, into the silence he left for her to fill, said, "Don't be. It was shortly after Grandma died. I guess I was scared of being alone so when Leo asked me, I married him. I expected we'd go on living here. He wasn't happy, though he found work quite readily. He was...restless. Bored with Mitikiltuk. We left."

She leaned her back against the counter and

gazed out the window behind Keith's head. He said nothing, only waited, a patient, half-expectant expression on his face.

"It turned out it wasn't Mitikiltuk that bored Leo, or any of the next half-dozen places we lived. It was me." She smiled to show him it didn't matter—which it didn't anymore. It had then, but didn't now.

"He found other women more interesting, more challenging."

As she resumed her seat, he leaned forward, arms on the table, gaze fixed on her face. A shaft of sunlight against the side of his face produced a squint, deepening the lines splaying out from the corners of his eyes. "Are you okay with it now?"

She felt he really wanted to know. "I'm fine with it. I think I was actually relieved to be able to come home, to settle in here instead of following someone else's dream the way I had during my childhood. I'd never intended to have a marriage like my mother's. I like stability."

"So you came home and started working at the library?"

"Yes. Part-time, at first, because I was looking afer my cousin Jake's little girls, then full-time as the assistant head librarian." Her voice wobbled and she quickly gulped the remains of her half-cold coffee, then set the cup back down on its saucer with a sharp click.

"Anyway," she said, squaring her shoulders, "I've had a busy life since then and I'm sure I'll have one without the library. I've become sort of an honorary maiden aunt to a lot of kids in the neighborhood, making myself available whenever their parents need a sitter on short notice. Maybe I'll open a day care."

"You like children."

Again, it wasn't a question, but she treated it as such. She nodded. "Very much. Jake—he's Cindy's older brother—lost his wife, leaving him with two toddlers. I raised them till Jake remarried."

He sat waiting, as if he expected her to add something to that. She frowned, looked down, listened to the old-fashioned coffee perk begin to glug, then glanced up again. He still sat there with that patient, watchful expression on his face. She cast around blindly for something to fill a silence that was becoming mildly uncomfortable.

She blinked. "I was happy for Jake and the kids, of course, and after that, I went to full-time at the library."

She looked at the front page of the newspaper and laughed lightly. "I'll find something to do." To her dismay, her voice cracked once more. Clearly she wasn't over the blow. Well, she'd just have to get over it, wouldn't she? She'd have to keep busy, keep her mind occupied until she did.

He nodded, but she could see the doubt in his eyes. She knew his skepticism was justified. But what was worse, was the pity she saw there, too. It was almost as if he knew her personal story as well as anyone in town.

She saw that same kind of pitying glance at every wedding she attended, at every christening, every time a neighbor saw her looking after someone else's children. *There she goes,* she could hear them saying silently, *poor, pathetic, old-maid librarian. Had her one chance and blew it for lack of the gumption to stick with her man and fight for what was rightfully hers.*

She cleared her throat. "Anyway, that seems to be the story of my life." She produced what she hoped was an insouciant grin. "Just when I get nicely into something, I'm rendered redundant."

He glanced at her quizzically. "But then, there's always the Galápagos Islands. You said something about next week?"

She tried to look bright, sound cheerful. "That's right. How long does it take to get a passport?"

"A little more than a week," he said dryly, "and longer than that to get permission to visit the Galápagos."

His expression said he doubted her competence to travel. And with good reason, she supposed. All her adult life had been spent right there in Mitikiltuk, except for the six months of her marriage, during which she'd been dragged from place to place by her husband. She'd made none of the plans, decided on none of the destinations, exactly as it had been during her childhood.

She wasn't even sure where to go to apply for a passport, so how could she even be considering travel as a means of escaping her problems? She felt tears prickle the backs of her eyes and stood quickly, gathering up the newspaper and rolling it tightly.

She managed another light laugh. "The Galápagos Islands thing was a joke," she said. "Just a crazy, momentary impulse, something to say, not something I ever mean to do."

"Why not? What's stopping you?"

She turned slowly and looked at him. Why not, indeed? What was stopping her? Hah! That answer, she knew. *Cowardice.*

"I wouldn't know how." She managed a light laugh. "Do you know, I have never even checked into a hotel on my own? How could I get on a flight to a foreign country, a place where I don't speak the language, don't know the ropes?"

Don't know the routine.

"And besides, I have people...relying on me."

"Who?"

He would ask. And then sit there waiting for an answer, silent, expectant, interested. *Caring.*

Who did rely on her? Not her parents—they were eminently self-sufficient, spending many months of the year in their motor home, traveling all over North America. Not any of her brothers, none of whom lived anywhere near. Not even any of her cousins anymore. Except maybe Cindy, who used her as a free dressmaker when her clothing needed alterations. And the neighbors, of course, to look after their children.

None of them ever hesitated to ask because they

all knew she never had any pressing engagements outside of work. If she sometimes felt a little, well, used, wasn't that better than having people ignore her existence entirely?

Maybe not.

Well, darn it, hadn't she decided already it was time for a change? A frisson of what might have been excitement, and might just as well have been terror, swept over her, much the same kind of emotion as Keith Devon's penetrating looks could evoke. Not to mention his quick little, hardly-there-at-all kisses that nevertheless had the power to make her heart race and her breathing become erratic.

"No one," she said. "No one at all relies on me for anything important, now there's no library."

"Then, if traveling's what you want, what's stopping you?"

"I don't know the first thing about it."

"Why not learn? You're a librarian. I bet you've helped lots of people research things. Research that for yourself, make all the necessary arrangements, then get on a plane and go visit the Galápagos Islands. In fact, it sounds like a fine idea to me. Maybe I'll even join you."

"Joey! You'll do nothing of the kind!"

They both twisted around. Mrs. Rathbury stood, hands on plump hips, face flushed, hair frazzled, as though Altar Guild duties had been particularly onerous that morning.

Keith smiled. "Aunt Ruth."

"Your father called me before you arrived and said you were overtired, stressed out and in desperate need of some peace and quiet. You are not, flatly *not,* going anywhere with anyone, let alone Alison."

"Why not Alison?" Keith asked, quite reasonably, Ali thought. What kind of objections could Mrs. Rathbury possibly have to her? She'd thought her neighbor liked her.

"Alison never goes anywhere, dear," Mrs. Rathbury explained kindly. "Hardly even to Kentonville unless she's forced. A real homebody, our Alison. Everyone knows that. That's why I asked her to come over and meet you, fix breakfast for you. I knew at once she'd be exactly what you need as a vacation companion—a quiet, unassuming, relaxing young woman who wouldn't add to your stress or make any untoward demands."

There could be no mistaking her meaning. "And maybe she could become so much more than a vacation companion."

She glanced at Ali. "The poor boy's been bouncing around from one war zone to another for years. His nerves are shot, stretched so tight he has fits at the sound of birdsong."

"Aunt Ruth, it wasn't birdsong, it was—"

"Now, don't interrupt me, Joey, dear. And don't contradict me. I distinctly recall your father's telling me about you and that silly bird last week. Why, you flung the poor man into a ditch and flopped down on him!"

"Not because the bird was *singing,* Aunt Ruth. It was a woodpecker hammering on a tree. It sounded like machine-gun fire. It was reflex that made me throw Dad into the ditch."

"Reflex? It was nerves. That's why you're here, and that's why you're staying. The Galápagos Islands, indeed. That's all you need, a bunch of Greeks shouting and gesturing and upsetting your equilibrium with their unintelligible babble. There are terrorists there, for goodness' sake!"

"The Galápagos Islands aren't in Greece, Aunt Ruth. They're—"

"I know perfectly well where they are—out of this country, and that's all that matters. It's also why you're not going there, if I have to chain you to the porch."

Mrs. Rathbury snorted and thumped her huge, tapestry handbag onto the table. It clanked as if it had chains in it.

"And that," she said with great finality, "is that. Now, sit down."

To Ali's amazement, Keith sat down.

"Why do you call him Joey?" The question popped out before Ali could remind herself that it was none of her business.

"Because he—"

"Aunt Ruth, please! That's embarrassing!"

"Nonsense, dear. It's a charming story. What's wrong with a four-year-old believing himself a kangaroo?"

She smiled, turning back to Ali. "He thought if

he tried hard enough to be a baby kangaroo, like the one in the Rolf Harris song, he'd be allowed to hitch a ride on Santa's sleigh all the way to Australia. Even then, the boy wanted to travel."

"Aunt Ruth, I didn't even have a clue that Australia involved travel. All I wanted was a ride on the sleigh!"

His great-aunt ignored him. "You should have seen him, hopping along everywhere he went. Why, that child didn't walk properly for almost two solid years. He bounced and amazingly, he actually looked like a kangaroo when he did it, those dear, dimpled little hands curled up against his chest, his legs bent as he bounded here, bounded there. His mother used to despair of his ever walking normally again, but of course he did."

Ali stared at Keith's large, brown, competent hands balled into fists on the table, and tried to visualize them half their size, pudgy, dimpled...*dear.* She laughed.

Keith glowered at her, at his aunt. "Thank you, Aunt Ruth. I'm sure Ali's grateful you shared that story."

"Now, don't be such a grump, darling. It is a charming story, isn't it, Alison?"

"Oh, yes, yes it is, Mrs. Rathbury," Ali said, biting her lip to stop herself from laughing.

Suddenly the old lady clapped her hand over her mouth and swung her gaze to Ali. "Oh, my dear. Speaking of stories! The most terrible news! I almost forgot, thinking about you and Joey going to

Greece together. The library. Alison, dear—'' she lovered her voice as if about to announce the demise of a beloved relative ''—I'm afraid the library's...gone. It burned down during the night. It was the talk of the church this morning.''

She patted Ali's hand. ''I'm so very sorry, because I know how you adored the place, but think of it this way, now you'll be free to show Joey around. There's a new motel out on the highway and I'm told their restaurant does a wonderful brunch. They have a chef from one of the big hotels in the city. Why don't you take him there right now?''

Ali groaned.

Keith looked at the ceiling for a moment before beginning to stack the dishes on the table.

''We've just finished breakfast,'' Ali said, rising to help Keith, but Mrs. Rathbury brushed her words aside impatiently.

''Don't be silly, Alison. It's almost noon. You must have had breakfast hours ago.''

Ali glanced at her watch, amazed to see the old lady was right. How long had she sat there, babbling on about her life? Poor Keith!

''I'm not hungry, and I'm sure your nephew has better things to do with a vaca—''

''I'm just as sure he hasn't,'' Mrs. Rathbury said, interrupting. ''You must get out and keep your mind off your worries. You'll need five minutes to change out of your gardening clothes, but then Joey will be at your front door. Won't you, Joey?"

It wasn't a request. It was an order.

Mrs. Rathbury clapped her hands as if Ali were one of the first-graders she'd spent half her lifetime teaching. "Now, run along."

As Ali headed out, she heard Mrs. Rathbury continue. "That one's *wife* material, my boy. See that you treat her with respect."

Ali whirled and marched back through the door. "If you are referring to me, Mrs. Rathbury, I am not wife material, even assuming your nephew was looking for one. I am also not going out for brunch. I've eaten two breakfasts already today. I am going home to finish weeding my carrots. In peace. And by myself! Is that clear?"

Two sets of eyes turned to her, stared at her. One mouth dropped open in surprise. One curved into a grin, and one voice boomed out in boisterous, male laughter.

"And then," Ali said loudly over top of the noise, "I am going to pack for my trip to Ecuador."

With that, she turned her back on their startled expressions and marched on home.

Behind her, she heard a pair of large, masculine hands applauding.

Oddly that only made her want to laugh.

She couldn't remember a morning when she'd had more fun.

4

KEITH FOLLOWED his aunt outside as she toddled after Ali.

"Oh, dear!" The old lady frowned at the gate Ali had slammed. "Alison's never impertinent. She must be having some kind of adverse reaction to the burning of the library."

Keith gazed at her. "You expected maybe a positive reaction?"

"Of course not. But Alison never slams anything and she just slammed the gate."

Keith was about to mention the cup, saucer and sugar bowl, but decided his aunt had had enough shocks for one morning.

"Go after her, Joey," Ruth pleaded. "She needs someone. The poor darling is so...alone."

Keith considered it. He more than considered it. He took two steps toward the gate, then came to a halt, frowning. Ali Kozinski was not his responsibility. She lived here in Mitikiltuk. She'd lived here for a long time. She'd mentioned parents, cousins, aunts, uncles, friends. How could she be alone?

"You can't let that innocent girl go scurrying off to Greece all by herself," Ruth said, fixing him with a severe glare. "You obviously spent the morning filling her head with dazzling stories of your foreign travels, so don't you think that makes you responsible for her safety?"

"Um, well, if you put it that way. I suppose I should go and try to talk her out of it." Anything would be better than trying to maintain a sober expression in the face of his aunt's lecture. Besides, he'd enjoyed Ali's company.

"Talk her *out* of it?" Ruth's eyes grew round with indignation behind her round glasses. "Whatever for? It would be the best thing that ever happened to her. Only she needs...guidance. You could go and discuss her plans with her, help her make them."

Keith discovered he was thinking about that, too, and all too eagerly. Hadn't Ali admitted to never having checked into a hotel by herself? Was she even equipped to recognize a safe place to stay, especially in a foreign land? Talk about an innocent abroad! He should never have suggested she make good on her threat to go to Ecuador!

Before he could comment, Ruth piped up again, face aglow with zeal. His great-aunt liked nothing better than making plans—especially for other people. "Why, you said yourself you might even go with her, and you're absolutely right. No woman should travel without a man for protection, and who better than a man well versed in the pitfalls of travel?"

She'd clearly forgotten her threat to chain him to the porch if he tried to leave the country again.

"Mrs. Rathbury!" came an indignant yelp, accompanied by a thump on the fence. "I do not need your nephew or any other man to guide me anywhere!"

Ruth hopped nimbly up into her wheelbarrow and leaned her head over the fence. "Alison, didn't your mother teach you about eavesdropping?"

Keith looked over the fence as Ali stood. His mouth dried up simply from watching her wipe her hands on the seat of her shorts. The action did incredible things to the front of her tank top. So as not to stare, he propped his elbows on the fence and gazed instead at the sun spangles on the golden tips of Ali's lashes. He'd never seen anyone's eyelashes look like that. Their dazzle mesmerized him. The whole world seemed to be holding its breath in that moment as he waited for Ali to blink again, dispensing showers of golden fairy dust.

Ali broke the spell. "Since I said I planned to weed the carrots," she said, her tone even and reasonable, "and you know perfectly well they're right beside the fence, you can scarcely accuse me of eavesdropping if you discuss me only two feet away."

"The lady has a point," Keith told his aunt, and grinned at Ali. He leaned over the fence, filched a raspberry from under a cluster of leaves at the top of a tall cane and popped it into his mouth. He licked the juice from his lips; the tip of Ali's pink tongue appeared for just an instant between hers.

He groaned, causing his aunt to look at him sharply. "What's wrong?"

"Nothing," he muttered. Deliberately he chose another raspberry, reached over and pressed it against Ali's lips, which parted in surprise as she accepted his offering. Her lower lip just barely grazed his finger, but still had an extraordinary effect on him.

Ali jerked back. Oh, Lord! What was she doing, standing there letting Keith Devon feed her raspberries, and right in front of his great-aunt?

To Ali's gratitude, her phone rang and she whirled, running inside to get it.

As she picked up the phone, she peeked out the window to see Keith still standing at the fence, only half-obscured by the tall raspberry canes. The canes wavered. He was still filching her berries. How could he possibly be hungry after the breakfast they'd consumed? But then, he was a tall man with a muscular physique; maybe that made the difference. Undoubtedly his appetite was much greater than hers.

She had sensed in him some very strong appetites indeed. Could feelings of hunger be catching? Could one person's appetites increase another's?

"That was a big sigh," Cindy said by way of greeting before Ali so much as said "Hello." Ali hadn't been aware of sighing. She dragged her gaze away from the window.

Luckily Cindy thought it had been occasioned by the devastation at the library, and offered her sympathy. Then, as she went on, describing her overnight sailing escapade, which included skinny-dipping and other delights, Ali was forced to acknowledge that Cindy would be much more suitable to deal with Keith Devon's appetites than she ever would. She sighed again, this time, silently, and when the conversation was over, determined to put the man right out of her mind. Forever.

MONDAY MORNING she was up as usual at half-past six. She drank her normal two cups of coffee, ate a peach fresh off the tree and a slice of toast, and tried not to remember the aroma of sizzling bacon from yesterday. She also tried not to remember how much she had enjoyed sharing the meal with Keith Devon. She wondered if he was awake yet, wondered what he would have for breakfast, and wondered, too, if his aunt was home to fix it for him.

Ridiculous! If Mrs. Rathbury was out, Keith could surely fend for himself. He was, after all, a grown man.

Yes… Oh, yes, indeed. He certainly was.

After a moment of standing and aimless staring, Ali wiped the smile off her face and scrubbed the bathroom floor. Then, she dusted all the lampshades, watered the houseplants and polished their leaves. That took only half an hour despite the way her muscles ached from cleaning all the kitchen cupboards the day before. She found other little make-work projects, but none of them lasted long enough or occupied more than her hands.

The fact was, she realized, she was not only bored with her own company, but she was also lonely. She needed to be among people, hear others' voices, see others' smiles. She needed her co-workers, needed her library regulars and occasionals alike.

This was nothing new, of course. She felt this way every year during her vacation. Vacations were periods to be dreaded, not anticipated with pleasure.

She wondered if Keith was enjoying his. Mitikiltuk, B.C., wasn't exactly a vacation paradise, especially for a single person.

The elderly came here, yes, to sit on the broad terraces of the Old Mitikiltuk Hotel overlooking the lake, and to play shuffleboard and lawn bowling. Though the hotel was getting as run-down as most of its visitors, they still continued to come. She wondered what they'd do if it ever sold to some up-and-coming developer who'd tear it down and build condos. It had been on the market for something like ten years now, so maybe it would never happen. For their sake, and the community's she hoped not. It was part of history, part of the establishment, part of what she saw as her roots.

Or was that just her, not wanting change?

Young families with children filled the government and private campgrounds as well as the amusement park; maybe they'd fill a more up-to-date hotel, as well, and turn Mitikiltuk into a livelier place.

Boaters pulled into the marina for fuel and supplies, but they never stayed long. There was nothing to stay for.

There was nothing worth doing here for a man like Keith Devon.

For that matter, there was nothing worth doing here for an unemployed librarian. Ali caught herself sighing again. Dammit, this self-pity simply had to stop! Activity. She just needed to keep busy.

She did have one very important errand to run today. She owed Mrs. Rathbury a bone china cup and saucer, which she wouldn't get in Mitikiltuk. She might get it in K'ville, so that was where she'd go. If not there, she'd drive on to Kamloops, maybe even Vancouver—Seattle—San Francisco. She laughed. "Quito!"

She could keep on going until she felt like turning back, even if that turned out to be days from now.

Or possibly not at all. As for work, she never had to work another day in her life unless she chose to. Her grandmother's legacy had seen to that.

She let herself out of the house, carefully locking the door behind her, struggling against the strangest impulse to go next door and say, "Good morning, Keith. I'm driving into K'ville. Would you like to come along? Just for something to do." She could be casual about it, friendly. Neighborly. There was nothing wrong with that, was there?

She had actually walked through the gate and into her neighbor's garden when she realized what she was doing. Keith hadn't looked any happier than she felt about being set up and she had news for Mrs. Rathbury. For Mrs. Rathbury's nephew, too: She did not chase men. Men didn't chase her, either, but that was beside the point. She wanted him to know she was not to be his vacation entertainment just because his aunt thought it was a good idea.

As silently as she'd arrived, Ali slipped away. She refused to make a fool of herself over a man who'd be in Mitikiltuk for a few weeks at best. Especially a man who had the kind of effect on her Keith Devon had.

Get going, Ali. You have things to do today.

And spending time with Keith Devon was not among them.

KEITH ROSE MUCH EARLIER than he'd planned. After lying in bed for half an hour past waking, telling himself he could learn to enjoy the luxury of it, he rolled out. Thirty minutes of inactivity were more than enough.

His aunt was out about her business, having left him a note. He checked the kitchen for food, and found nothing appealing. At least, nothing as appealing as he'd found there the previous morning. He put that thought firmly behind him.

Determined to make the most of his vacation and do as his dad had ordered—"relax"—he munched a muffin and a banana, then slugged back a cup of coffee, refilled his mug and strolled outside with it. He wandered through the garden, the sun baking down on his bare shoulders, feeling good. He even stopped and smelled a rose, pale yellow, verging on cream.

It reminded him of Ali's hair: soft, delicate and almost iridescently gold.

He glanced at the fence and wondered if she was weeding her carrots and would like company. She wasn't. What did an unemployed librarian do after the carrots were weeded?

He filched another raspberry or two and walked back toward the house. Stroking the rose petals again, he remembered how the velvet touch of her lower lip against his finger had nearly sent him into orbit. Spending time with Ali Kozinski was not the way to relax.

Trouble was, whether he liked it or not, he had a bad case of Ali-on-the-mind, and didn't know what to do about it. One thing he did know, sitting around and thinking about her was not the way to get past this temporary obsession of his.

Action. That's what he needed, and a change of scene.

After changing into jeans and a T-shirt, he left a note for his aunt. "Off to K'ville. Expect me when you see me."

In his hurry to get away, he nearly backed his bronze Bronco into Ali's sea green Cavalier as she backed out of her garage.

Her hair all pulled up tight in her bun, she offered him a vague smile and the kind of unenthusiastic wave practised by royalty.

He drove north around the crescent, she drove south, and to his surprise, when he swung onto the main road leading to the heart of Mitikiltuk, there was Ali's car right ahead of him.

He grinned, seeing her license plate: BOOKS. He wouldn't have pegged Ali Kozinski as one for vanity plates, but there it was. Just went to show what he actually knew about the woman.

Nothing. Zip. And that was the way to keep it.

Except...she smelled good.

Hell, lots of women smelled good. That was no excuse for going overboard.

And, well, she'd felt good against his body.

Yeah? And so what?

And so he experienced disappointment out of all proportion when, instead of carrying on through Mitikiltuk and heading for Kentonville, she made a right turn into the drugstore parking lot and disappeared from sight.

Keith stopped on the outskirts of town and gassed up. As he was about to go inside to pay, he caught sight of a sea green Cavalier zipping by, headed for K'ville.

Well! Was it Ali? The man behind the counter was painfully slow when it came to processing Keith's credit card, and by the time he was back on the highway, of course there was little hope of catching Ali. If it had been her at all. And why would he want to catch her?

To unpin her hair.

What the hell? He didn't give a damn about Ali Kozinski's hair! Or her whereabouts. Today, he had other unexplored territory to check out.

EVEN BEFORE SHE REACHED the block where the library had stood, Ali smelled the acrid scent of its destruction. Unable to bear the thought of seeing it, she swung into the drugstore parking lot, out the back entrance and along the alley to the next block, which took her safely past, and back onto the highway two blocks farther on.

In Kentonville, she went first to the library to make an appointment for an interview with Katerina Boyd, director of the library and her only real hope of employment. Doubtful, she gazed around the main area, wondering if she'd ever be happy in such a sterile, modern establishment. Assuming they were even hiring.

As a cover for her casing the place, she picked up several brochures all neatly arrayed in little pockets on a wall stand, glanced at them without seeing them and stuffed them into her purse. It was too quiet in the library. The junior section had no children, no moms, no grandmotherly volunteers reading to groups of kids. She couldn't see a colorful travel poster anywhere on any of the off-white walls, the way she'd had them adorning the dark panels of her library.

How could she consider working there? Yet, if the opportunity arose, how could she consider not taking it? She had to do something, didn't she?

Yes, she did, if only to protect her sanity. It was this library or no library at all, because, let's face it, Ali, she told herself disparagingly, Kentonville is about as far as you're ever going to go from Mitikiltuk again. All the tempting travel posters she'd put up on the walls of her library had ever really tempted *her* to do was read books about foreign, exotic places.

And make unexpected, wildly untrue statements about her future plans. She knew in her heart of hearts that all her talk of travel had as much substance as the threat of a child in a snit to run away from home.

Reluctantly she approached the circular central counter, behind which a woman sat at a computer terminal, under a hanging sign reading Information.

The woman glanced up. "Hello," she said. "May I help you?" She sounded pleasant enough, but to Ali's ears, her voice lacked sincerity and she certainly detected no warmth in the other's face. It was as if Ali had interrupted something far more important than waiting on a mere customer.

"I, uh, yes. I—" Ali broke off as the other woman stood, coming to the counter. Suddenly she felt as if she were a country cousin in her cotton skirt and blouse. However appropriate her clothing might have been in *her* library, they didn't cut it here. However neat and well pressed they might have been when she left home, she knew they were wrinkled from the heat, and in them she felt less than businesslike, less suited for a job interview than for a rummage sale. As one of the items up for grabs.

Dressed in a pale blue silk suit with a pleated blouse that had a little back bow tucked under the collar, the other woman looked sophisticated, cool, professional and as daunting as the rest of the library.

"I'd like to see Mrs. B-Boyd." Ali cursed the stutter that plagued her when she felt most insecure. "I mean, maybe not *see* her, but I'm here to, um..." She tried to steady her hands as she reached into her shoulder bag for her résumé.

The woman glanced at the paper Ali withdrew and waved toward the end of the room. "Up there. Room M-5, down the corridor to your left at the top of the stairs." She tilted one eyebrow up. "I'm sure you'll enjoy it. And benefit from it, too."

Before Ali could ask "Enjoy what?" the woman smiled intimately at a man who had just come in and stood leaning casually on the counter. She seemed to have forgotten Ali was even there.

Ali drew a deep breath and ascended the broad, shallow flight of stairs to the mezzanine.

At the room marked M-5, she stood and frowned at the sign on the open door: Assertiveness Training Seminar, 1:00 p.m.—4:00 p.m. Katerina Boyd. She glanced down at the paper she still held in her hand and saw, not the résumé she thought she'd been offering the receptionist, but one of the brochures she'd picked at random off the rack.

Perhaps twenty other women sat at tables facing the front of the room where Mrs. Boyd stood, chalk in hand, saying, "...not rudeness, not agressiveness. Assertiveness is about politely, but firmly, stating your case in terms that make it clear you intend to get what you want and refuse to permit others to obstruct you unnecessarily. It's about not accepting substandard treatment or patronization from anyone. This can be accomplished in many—"

She broke off, noticing her students' attention more on the doorway than on herself.

"Well, hello there," she said with a smile, "come on in. Everyone's welcome in this room. Find yourself a chair."

Ali had met the woman once, during her brief visit following the new library's opening. Now, though, the older woman didn't appear to recognize her. She wasn't surprised; she knew she was eminently forgettable.

She'd never be sure why she did it, but instead of saying it was a mistake, her showing up there, Ali sidled into the room hesitantly, aiming at a vacant chair at the back of the room.

"No, no. Stop right there," said Mrs. Boyd. Ali froze, wondering what in the world she had done wrong. She had a swift vision of Keith Devon laughing at her for thinking she could travel, laughing at her for blushing, and knew she was doing it now. She was deeply grateful he wasn't here to witness whatever fiasco she had gotten herself into during something no more adventurous than a trip to the Kentonville Library.

DESPITE THE NOTE he'd left for his aunt, Keith passed right on through Kentonville's unprepossessing downtown core.

For several hours, he drove aimlessly, along wide, well-traveled highways, along narrow, dirt tracks leading in winding puzzles around steep-sided hills, or across open fields. He looked up mountains, down into gorges and traced the wandering tracks of minor rivers until he scarcely knew where he was.

No one shot at him. No bombs went off in the distance. No military checkpoints barred his way.

He even took out his favorite camera and shot off a few frames at scenes that appealed to him. Not a single one contained a dead body. Not a single one would be of the slightest interest to his editor at *ActionBeat*.

However, they fascinated him: The peace of an ancient, weathered barn with a clump of dandelions growing inexplicably on one corner of the roof; the reflection of a brown-eyed Susan in a still stretch of a stream; the quiet serenity of a gray horse lying in green grass under the shade of a poplar tree.

He stopped for a hamburger in a little place with one gas station, one small store and a grubby café. The burger was good, the fries made with fresh potatoes with the skins on and the accompanying milk shake was almost too thick to pull up through the straw. Yet when he left that town and headed back toward Mitikiltuk, he felt unsatisfied, as if he'd been searching for something and had failed to find it.

The minute he found it, though, he knew.

There it was. Ali's sea green car parked on a side street just off the main drag in Kentonville. He felt a big, stupid grin crease his face as he swung to the curb of the street at right angles to where Ali had parked, hopped out and stuffed coins into a meter.

Then, stuffing his fingers into the back pockets of his jeans, he strolled along, checking store windows. When he found her, wherever she might be, he wanted to appear casual, not as if he'd located a deposit of diamonds. Not as if his pulse had begun to race at the sight of her car.

Now all he needed to know was, where was Ali?

ALI STOOD RIGID just inside the door to the classroom. Katerina Boyd strode toward her. "Now," she said, "everyone, watch, and remember this is the way to enter a room."

From Ali's side, she smiled at the assembled women, gave them a brief nod of greeting and strode briskly across the room. To do so, she had to walk in front of everyone there, and she did it without blushing, without hesitating, without slinking along a wall, and without keeping her head down in an attempt to remain invisible. She gracefully took a seat and uncapped the pen that lay before her on a blank notebook.

After a moment, she stood and returned to the podium. Then she said to Ali, "Now, you do it. Remember, you have a right to be here. You're wanted here. You're important to this group. Join us."

To her amazement, Ali did, omitting only the confident smile. To her further amazement, everyone joined Mrs. Boyd in applauding her.

"Now, what's your name? Just stand, face the group and give us your first name only today and a very brief statement on how you feel about being here. Everyone is shy, but that won't last."

"My name is Ali." She wondered if she was supposed to add something like "and I'm an alcoholic," but since she wasn't, and since this was an assertiveness training seminar and she thought a positive statement would be appropriate, she only added, "I'm glad to be here."

At five minutes past four, Katerina Boyd answered the last of many questions her audience had fired at her. Ali sat, awed by admiration.

Who would ever have thought the woman had spent nearly ten years virtually trapped in her own home by panic attacks? She evinced such strength of character, such self-confidence, such...ease. When she spoke, everyone listened.

"That's all for today, ladies. You have all come here in the hope of reinventing yourself, and you are all going to succeed. We'll take it in easy stages. You all know what frightens you most. List those things, things you'd like to do, but are afraid to try. Next week, we'll discuss it further, and break the lists down to the five most important factors for each of you. Five changes you think you can make in your life."

"I'll leave you with one thought—Eleanor Roosevelt once said, 'No one can make you feel inferior without your consent.' Remember that, and you'll be well on the road toward achieving the goals each of you will be setting for herself in the next session."

Ali lifted her head and held it high as she left the library. Goals? She wondered what those would be, once she thought of it. She was good at setting goals, making lists. It was part of her logical, routine-oriented personality. She could do it. She would do it. She would reinvent Alison Kozinski.

She could do anything she wanted to do. All she had to do was remember her own worth. If she didn't recognize it, no one else would. And if she wanted to go to the Galápagos Islands, then by gosh, that's where she'd go!

A glance at her watch told her she still had plenty of time before the travel agency closed.

She hurried over to the travel agency, filled out her passport application, took it to a pharmacist around the corner who had known her for some time and had him endorse it. She returned to the agency and collected several pamphlets, plus a visa application that she could send in with her passport documents. It would all take only a few days, she was assured, with the new system in place.

Ali carefully tucked all her new, exciting literature into her shoulder bag and almost floated out of the travel agent's office.

Life of adventure, here I come.

But before she went running off to Ecuador and the Galápagos Islands, she had one important errand to take care of. She owed Mrs. Rathbury one bone china cup and saucer set.

5

NOT FAR from the Kentonville Library, Ali went straight to a store called the Glass House, sure they'd have exactly what she wanted.

The door swung open. She walked though, half-blind before her eyes adjusted, and ran smack into a very solid figure. "Hold it," said a warm, familiar voice, and she nearly moaned aloud as his arms came around her, holding her. "This isn't the kind of place you want to go blundering in to."

As Ali drew a deep breath laden with the essence of Keith, her hands went to his shoulders to steady herself. "Yes, it is," she said. "This is exactly where I wanted to be."

He grinned, his hands encircling her waist. "In my arms? Does this mean you were following me, hoping for just such an opportunity? I like your style, Ali, but what do you say we find a bit of privacy?"

Ali groaned as she jerked out of his hold, heat burning in her face. "In your— I didn't say that!"

He laughed softly. "That's what it sounded like to me, and if it's not what you meant, why are you blushing so red?"

"If I'm blushing, it's because that's *not* what I

meant. I mean, I intended to come to this store, not to blunder into your, er, into you. I wasn't following you! I didn't even know you were here! I like this store. The *store* is where I wanted to be. Not your arms and...I..."

Good grief! So much for assertiveness training! She was sure it didn't permit senseless babbling and fiery blushing. It demanded cool coherence, taking the initiative, which she attempted.

"What are *you* doing here, anyway?"

"I came in looking for you, as a matter of fact, but the place is full of so many breakables, and the saleswoman followed me as if she thought I was going to stuff priceless goblets into my pockets, so I bought this, and scrammed."

"This" was an object in a plastic bag. "It's for you."

He slipped an arm around her waist and moved her out of the doorway so some other shoppers could enter. His touch again created a bubbling, exciting sensation in her tummy, and curved her lips into a smile she couldn't wipe off. Oh, help! He did such weird things to her mind, her self-control.

"For me?"

"Well, not exactly," he admitted. "It's a cup and saucer for you to give to Aunt Ruth. Genuine *Blossom Time* pattern."

He slid the handles of the bag over her hand and onto her wrist, patted it there and let her hand go. "A gift from me to you."

"I—" Ali stared at him in confusion. "But I was coming here to buy this myself." Confusion gave way to indignation. "Did you think I wouldn't?"

His smile made her insides do an uncomfortable flip-flop. "I knew you would. So I decided to beat you to it."

Ali's eyes narrowed slightly with suspicion as she took half a step back from him. "Why?"

Yeah, why? Keith asked himself even as he shrugged and shortened the distance she'd put between them. What was he going to say? *Because your eyes are blue? Because I like the way you smell? Because you feel good in my arms?* He didn't suppose she'd want to hear any of those reasons, all of which were true, but none of which came even close to explaining why he'd done it. He couldn't even explain it adequately to himself.

"Because I felt like it," he said. "And because I suspect you're going to have to watch your pennies until you get another job."

"Oh, Keith..." To his consternation, tears glimmered in her eyes and he rushed on before she could say another word.

"Besides, you were kind enough to come rushing over at a moment's notice to 'baby-sit' a neighbor's poor little nephew so he wouldn't have to wake up alone in a strange house, so consider it a child-care fee."

Ali surprised him by laughing, while those tears of hers sort of splashed around, sparkling in the sun until they were gone. It was a captivating sight. She surprised him further by not arguing. "All right," she said. "Thank you. On that basis, I accept your gift."

He grinned at her in amazed delight, having to suppress a strong desire to sweep her into his arms and give her a hug to end all hugs. He'd been certain she'd get all huffy and stiff and argue the point, insist on paying him back for the cup and saucer, asserting her independence. Whereupon he'd have to get even stiffer and huffier, asserting his masculinity, and they'd probably end up arguing angrily, with one or both of them stomping off in a temper, which would likely mean the end of whatever kind of friendship they might be about to develop.

Hell, maybe that wasn't such a bad idea. Offend her so she'd make a point of staying away from him since he seemed incapable of forcing himself to stay away from her?

If it had been his intention—even unconsciously—it had backfired. For a self-confessed routine-junkie, the woman did a remarkable number of unexpected things.

More than ever, he wanted to be around for the next surprise.

"Since this 'poor boy' was sentenced to wake up all alone in a strange house this morning, without a pretty blond baby-sitter to comfort him, and since he had to have a hamburger for lunch all alone in a greasy spoon somewhere out back of beyond, how about joining him for dinner?'' he asked.

Then, with a grin, added, ''I hear there's this new place out on the highway and they have a great chef. I'm sure Aunt Ruth would expect me to take you there, since we met here in town.''

Ali's face, her entire personality, closed off from him in the next instant. It was like watching the sun go behind a cloud, and then seeing lightning flash. He almost held his breath waiting for the boom of thunder.

Instead she just said ''No. No, thank you,'' but he knew she was angry enough to throw dishes. ''You needn't feel obliged to ask me out, Keith Devon. I'm quite capable of selecting my own dinner partners if and when I want one.''

Before he could recover, she'd scurried away to her car, jaywalking, jay*running,* which he considered was probably completely out of character for her and indicative of her agitation. As was his chasing after her indicative of his confusion, but he did that anyway. Though he leaped in front of a taxi, all but vaulting its hood, earning himself a rude blast from its horn, Ali was inside her car and pulling out dangerously close in front of a pickup truck before he was halfway across the street.

She drove off without looking back, leaving him to stare after her, wondering just what in hell had happened from one instant to the next.

What had he done? What had he said?

Striding angrily back to his Bronco, he replayed

their converstation, but could pinpoint no words she might have misconstrued as an insult.

Damn, but she was one confusing woman. Still, hadn't he just told himself he liked suprises? Yeah, but not unpleasant ones. Keith got into his vehicle and shut the door. He might as well go on home.

WHAT HAD SHE BEEN THINKING of? Ali asked herself for the hundredth time as she drove hard for home, just barely within the speed limit. Obviously she hadn't been thinking, period. She'd been reacting. Responding. With gratitude, of all things because the man was thoughtful and caring enough to worry about her being unable to afford to replace the broken cup.

Clearly Mrs. Rathbury hadn't told Keith a thing about Ali's financial status, nor that she'd done her library job almost as a volunteer, accepting only a tiny stipend to keep things legal because she didn't need money. She'd been more touched than she'd expected to be at his gesture in trying to save her a few dollars because she was out of work.

She would, at that point, probably have followed him into a war zone, until he reminded her that his aunt was the one who had suggested he take her out to the new place on the highway. His invitation to dinner had been motivated by nothing more than a desire to please his aunt.

She stiffened her back and shoulders. *Now, cut that out!* Maybe it hadn't been. Maybe he really had wanted to have dinner with her because he wanted her company? What had she done?

She'd been unforgivably rude, that's what!

If that was what recreating herself was going to mean, maybe she'd better decide to stay just the way she was, plain, staid, Ali Kozinski who never got mad at anyone.

Anyone except Keith Devon, for some reason. Well, the mayor, too, she reminded herself, but she'd never gotten mad at him to his face. She'd never felt hurt enough to burst out with rude remarks and curt refusals. Obviously the way she reacted to him told her Keith was the kind of man she should avoid until she was a whole lot more sure of herself. The kind of man to forget about. Completely and permanently.

Though maybe not at once.

She sighed, wishing she hadn't talked so much on Sunday. Maybe if she'd acted in her more characteristically shy-mouse manner, she would have heard all his "dazzling tales" about world travel, and been able to pick his brains.

Damn, but he must have led an exciting life! And the exotic, foreign women he must have met... Jetsetters, sophisticates, royalty, probably, and maybe even spies! Women completely unlike herself.

Face it, Ali, you don't stand a chance at competing against women like that.

"I don't want a chance!" she all but shouted, slamming on the brakes as she nearly drove through the one traffic signal Mitikiltuk boasted. A horn honked behind her. She looked up to see that darned bronze Bronco practically on her rear bumper. The driver's door flew open, Keith leaped out and before she could react, he'd jerked open her door.

"Now, what was that all about?" he demanded.

Assertiveness deserting her, Ali's mouth opened and closed several times. The light turned green. Horns honked behind them. Keith ignored everything but her.

"I asked you to have dinner with me, not knock over the bank with me, or go to bed with me. There's a hotel right across the intersection. Promise me you'll pull into its parking lot and have dinner with me there or we'll stay here with traffic piling up behind us until someone calls the cops.

"Now won't that look good in the *Sunday News?*" he went on relentlessly. "Mitikiltuk's ex-head librarian has fight with boyfriend and stops traffic on Main Street during rush hour."

Ali gulped. "You're not my—"

"They won't know that."

She could have told him "they" would most certainly know that. Ali Kozinski didn't have dates, she didn't have boyfriends, she didn't even have a real life. More horns honked, more angrily, drivers got out of their cars to see what the holdup was. Even people on the sidewalk stopped and stared.

Ali nodded her agreement then realized she couldn't go anywhere even after Keith closed her door and returned to his own vehicle because the light was red again. As soon as it turned green, she drove through, still with him right on her bumper and pulled into the parking lot beside the Old Mitikiltuk Hotel.

Fine. If he insisted on having dinner surrounded by people with blue hair or no hair, she'd accommodate him. For sure he wouldn't like overdone broccoli and lumpy mashed potatoes or fatty prime rib, which was about the best the hotel offered in the way of dinners. Besides, the portions were small, since they were geared to serving seniors. He'd leave there hungry.

Hungry and humbled, she hoped. Once he was properly humbled, and sorry he'd insisted, she'd put her newly gained assertiveness to the test and tell him if he ever bullied her like that again, she'd let someone call the cops and put her picture in the paper. Hah! She'd show him!

Before getting out of her car, she took out her notebook and wrote down the first of her list of goals: "Don't let Keith Devon bully me again."

It would certainly do for a beginning. And what was it Katerina had said, quoting Eleanor Roosevelt? "No one can make you feel inferior without your consent." It could also apply to letting people intimidate her.

TO ALI'S UTTER DISGUST, Keith was charm personified as he opened her door, handed her out of the car as if she were as fragile as the cup and saucer all packaged up on the seat beside her. As the hostess, Mary Evans, seated them at a table overlooking the window, and handed them menus, Keith's charm persisted. Though Ali felt obliged to introduce him to Mary, and remark that he was visiting Ruth Rathbury, he scarcely even glanced at the hostess, who did her best to attract his attention.

Men always looked at Mary Evans, who had long, wavy red hair, dramatically made-up eyes and a full, pouting lower lip as voluptuous as the rest of her body. Tonight, as usual, she showed more cleavage than Ali even had.

Keith didn't appear to notice.

To Ali's further discombobulation, the menu had been changed and there was a delightful choice of meals from swordfish to rack of lamb. She ordered the first, Keith ordered the second, plus a bottle of sauvignon blanc. The food was well prepared and plentiful, the wine just right, and the deepening twilight made magical by the flickering torches surrounding the terrace beyond their window.

Ali kept wishing it was a *real* date, and that she was wearing something besides a cotton skirt and blouse and her favorite, if slightly scruffy, flat-soled sandals. At least it wasn't Saturday, so the old-fashioned band with its old-fashioned music wasn't on the bandstand; Keith wouldn't feel obliged to ask her to dance.

He kept up the conversation, telling her of more of his adventures all over the world, and she admitted to having put in her passport application that day. He congratulated her, then asked her what she knew of the Old Mitikiltuk Hotel and its history.

Luckily, it was a question she'd been asked many times by tourists and had all but memorized the book someone had written on it several years ago. Once more, she found it easy to respond to his manner of asking a question then going silent ans watchful as he waited for her reply.

Mary came by to ask if everything was all right with their meal, and did they need anything else, and overheard one of Ali's replies to one of Keith's questions.

"Are you interested in old buildings?" she asked, fixing her intense gray gaze on his face. Keith looked up, seeming to really notice Mary for the first time. Ali felt herself fade into the woodwork.

"Yes, I am," he said.

"I know the owner, and can get you a tour any time you like," Mary offered.

Keith looked at Ali. "Would you like that, or have you been through the place so many times it would bore you to death?"

"Oh, not tonight," Mary said quickly. "The owner's not in just now. It would be better if we did it on my day off, then I could show you around myself." Somehow, her words or manner made it perfectly clear the "you" did not include Ali.

"I'll call you at your aunt's place and we can set something up. Okay?"

IT WAS KEITH'S SMILE at Mary and his nod of agreement that Ali saw as she drove home with Keith's vehicle close behind her. Clearly Mary Evans had no trouble setting goals at a moment's notice, and her most obvious one was seducing Keith. Well, and what was to stop Ali from setting that as one of her goals, too, though it would be madly crazy, terrifyingly daring, trying to seduce Keith Devon.

Terrifyingly daring were the operative words there. She didn't even want to think about it.

Face it, Ali, she told herself, *you don't stand a chance at competing against a woman like Mary, either.*

"I don't want a chance!" she all but shouted, driving into her carport. She pulled on the handbrake with unnecessary vigor. "This is not a competition!"

Oh, really?

Yes, really!

She didn't even want to think about it. Keith Devon was not in her destiny. Weeding the pea patch was. At least until her passport came.

Still, over the next several days, she spent more time than she liked glancing at the road in front of her neighbor's house, noting the comings and goings of a certain bronze Bronco.

It was during one of its absences she had taken the cup and saucer along with her apology to Mrs. Rathbury, who claimed not to have noticed the lack of one cup and saucer.

Keith hadn't told his aunt about Ali's tantrum? Damn! The thought made her go all soft and gooshy inside. Why should the thought of being with him terrify her? He was a nice man, a good man.

Except, he was a nice man on vacation, exactly like Leo had been.

So? Wasn't she also considering a life of multiple vacations, just as soon as she developed the courage to make the first move? Maybe in her world travels, she'd meet up with Keith, on his world travels, and they could join up together for a day or two. Or three. Or a night or two or six.

The thought made her tingle all over.

The next time she visited Mrs. Rathbury's after seeing Keith's car disappear, her neighbor urged Ali to stay for a few minutes. Keith, she said, would be back soon. He'd just run to the store for a couple more books to read. He liked adventure stories, and history, and architecture. He'd even had a tour of the Old Mitikiltuk Hotel.

Maybe Ali had some books he could read. Mrs. Rathbury was sure he'd look after them and treat them well. If she didn't have time to stay now, Ali could call him later and invite him over to examine her bookcases.

Ali wondered if he'd equate "bookcases" with "etchings" and if he did, instead of saying *Are you following me, Ali?* he'd say, *Are you chasing me, Ali?*

And being the new, bold Ali, she'd smile and

say, "Why, yes, Keith, as a matter of fact, I am. How about we have a little vacation fling, just to get me geared up for all the lovely, dangerous foreign men I'm going to meet when I start traveling?"

Yet, when he arrived one morning to ask if she'd like to go for a swim, instead of saying she'd love to, she claimed she was just heading out the door to visit her mother.

He shrugged, smiled and said, "Another time, then."

Ali hurriedly went to visit her mother, so as not to make a liar out of herself, as well as a coward. But all she could think of as she drove across town was the pearly white untanned part of Keith Devon's backside that had told her unequivocally that his swim trunks were scarcely decent.

A few days later she heard in the post office that Mary Evans was making quite a play for Ruth Rathbury's visiting great-nephew.

Well! That certainly let her off the hook, didn't it? Mary Evans was everything Ali was not, and even had two little boys badly in need of some firm male guidance. Which reminded her of another thing to add to her list of goals. Talk to Mary about disciplining those two little boys.

KEITH WOKE UP much, much, too early on the second Thursday morning of his vacation, he thought as he sat on the end of the dock. What in hell was he doing up at dawn? He should be sleeping, but he was right back to his old, prevacation pattern of existing on dream-filled catnaps, then rising and pacing because restlessness and nightmares drove him from his bed.

That, and the possiblity of catching Ali unawares. Like it or not, she had intrigued him.

Once, he heard her humming as she did something in her garden, and was about to open the gate and stroll over just to chat, when the phone rang inside her house. Seconds later, her screen door slammed and he didn't hear a sound from her for the next two days.

On his way to the dock this morning, he'd even looked over the fence, hoping to find her weeding her precious vegetable garden, but there was no sign of her. Her drapes were closed. Maybe she had actually gone away, or maybe this was too early for even Ali to be up.

It was certainly too early for him. Still, instead of retreating to his bed, he laid down his book and pulled in deep, appreciative breaths laden with the scent of the lake. It reminded him of being six and on a tadpole hunt with his brother Dan.

No troubles at that age, no worries. No women. Just him and Dan splashing gleefully in the shallows and sloughs at the lake's edge. Keith and Dan and tadpoles…

Tadpole. Right. There had been a little catboat of that name here when he and Dan were kids. Was it still around? What shape would it be in after all these years?

Closing his eyes, he recalled the sailboat he'd seen on Saturday night, almost heard again the carefree laughter of the woman aboard it.

Maybe that was something Ali would enjoy. Maybe that would tempt her into his presence. In his opinion, sailing, like meals, should be shared, and though she'd refused to have lunch with him, or dinner, maybe she wouldn't refuse the other. After all, being outdoors in the sunshine wouldn't make it appear to be an intimate kind of date.

Oh, no?

A picture formed behind his closed lids. Ali, with sunshine spangling her lashes. Of course, she'd have her hair pulled back into that tight little librarian bun of hers. He felt a laugh begin way deep inside and let it rumble out. No problem. He'd slip that bun loose with his fingers, let the wisps curl against his throat, breathe in the perfume of it and—

He shot to his feet. Enough was enough! If *Tadpole* was still there, he'd get her fixed up and spend the rest of his vacation on the water. Alone.

He needed action. And he didn't need the company of any prim librarian who'd blush like a thirteen-year-old if she guessed even half of what she made him think.

Not even if she was a prim librarian with gold-tipped lashes and an unexpected flair for unexpected passion.

ON THE FAR SIDE of the point across the bay, Ali enjoyed a leisurely soak in the warm water, floating on her back with her eyes closed, wiggling fingers and feet only enough to stay afloat.

As the sun rose, creating a red curtain over her eyelids, she turned to her front and swam back around the point, then headed across the bay. She had just waded out of the water and picked up her towel, when a loud grunt and a scraping sound jerked her around.

There, like an enormous turtle with only one set of legs, came an upside-down boat, staggering down the sand. A pair of large, male feet splashed into the water and, with another grunt and a heave, the boat flopped keel-down into the shallows, parallel to the beach.

Ali stared as Keith, his back to her, grabbed its bow and heaved it farther out.

Ripples circled away, lapping up against the dock.

The sun shone on the gleaming skin of his back, enriching the brown of his suntan. The muscles in his legs and shoulders undulated as he waded around to tug the blunt stern of the boat several feet deeper. He slogged back around, grasped the bow again and heaved it out another few feet, soaking himself with an arching, rainbowed splash.

She finally let out a long, unsteady breath she hadn't been aware of holding. Lord, but he was something! Her knees went weak and her insides fluttered. She wanted him with an intensity she'd never before experienced.

Was this the result of one session of two assertiveness training sessions and a half-completed list of goals? Had it turned her into a sexual monster who was going to attack attractive men just to prove to herself she could?

No. Of course not. Katerina had made it clear that assertiveness had nothing to do with being aggressive, just positive about what she wanted.

It would help, though, to feel more positive that he'd think she was confident.

He crouched by the little craft, pushing one side of it under, as if trying to sink it.

Ali couldn't help herself. Her bare feet soundless in the soft sand, she crossed the ten yards that separated her from Keith. Wouldn't Katerina Boyd be proud!

"Good morning," she said. "Are you drowning that poor little boat?"

6

IF HER ARRIVAL startled him, he hid it well as he turned his head without rising. "Damn right," he said, deadpan. "My mother was frightened by a boat during her pregnancy with me so now every time I see one, I have an irresistible urge to sink it."

She approached closer, so close her toes caught the wavelets his efforts sent ashore. "Well, don't just stand there," he said, rocking the boat harder to slop more water inside it. "Can't you see I need help? This sucker has a real will to live."

Ali had to laugh as he pretended the boat was fighting back, threatening to swamp him. "Then maybe you should let it drift away gracefully and find another home."

"Never," he vowed. "This thing's dangerous. It's been lurking in the rafters of Aunt Ruth's garage, waiting for an opportunity to scare her—" he narrowed a gaze at Ali "—or any other unsuspecting woman who chances by. Maybe even you."

"Not me," Ali lied. "I don't scare easily."

He grinned as if he recognized her fib for what

it was, and she spoke up quickly before he could comment.

"Tadpole?" she said, reading the faded name on the little craft. "You're murdering a boat that someone cared about enough to give a name? Isn't that something like hunting down Bambi?"

"Nah." Keith had to smile at her serious face. A sudden and powerful need to reassure her that he was a nice guy flooded unexpectedly through him. It was important she know that.

"I'd never hurt a Bambi," he said, "and I'd never scuttle a boat unnecessarily. *Tadpole*'s been on dry land so long her planks have shrunk. She needs to soak so she won't leak quite so badly."

He stopped sloshing water into the boat and carried a line ashore, tying it to a secure post imbedded in the sand. As he turned to face her, he caught a glimpse of laughter lurking behind her gold-tipped lashes.

So she'd been kidding, despite the solemn face and earnest qucstion. Why hadn't he recognized that right off? Because he was taking her much too seriously?

He liked the subtlety of her humor, liked not knowing for sure when she was in earnest. He also liked very much the way she looked in a swimsuit, even if it was a one-piece thing lacking the usual high-cut legs and low-cut top. She looked just as sexy as if she were in a string bikini. Maybe more.

"I've decided to make her renovation one of my vacation projects."

Surprise crossed her face along with a quick smile that revealed a dimple at the right corner of her mouth. "I always have a vacation project, too. It makes the time go faster."

"Don't you like vacations?"

She shrugged. "Not especially. I always find them...lonely."

Okay, she'd given him the perfect opening.

"If you know about lonely vacations, how come you've been avoiding me?" he said in a husky voice.

He watched her chin tilt up, saw a glint of denial flicker across her eyes, then she gave her head a quick shake as if rejecting the impulse to lie.

"Because your aunt keeps trying to push us together," she said.

"That bothers you?"

Her mouth parted in swift surprise. "Well, of course it bothers me! I hate being 'fixed up.' Everyone in town does it to me all the time because they see me as an object of pity, a woman who couldn't hold her man, a woman who had to come slinking home and raise her cousin's babies instead of her own. I hate knowing you only asked me out because your aunt told you to."

He pulled in a deep breath and kept his gaze focused on hers. He didn't remember making a conscious decision that it was pointless trying to keep her out of his thoughts, out of his life, but now was the time to admit it. "That wasn't why I asked you out. I did it because I wanted to be with you, to share my time with you. To have some pleasant...company.''

She looked down quickly, then up again, slowly. ''Are you...have *you* been...lonely?''

Jeez! Did she have any idea what that kind of fluttery, unconsciously flirtatious look could do to a guy?

''Yes,'' he said, his voice raspy. Quickly he waded back out into the lake and crouched beside the boat, spilling more water into the hull.

''But I heard you were seeing Mary Evans.''

''You introduced us, she showed me through the hotel and I bought her lunch as a way of saying thanks. She's phoned me a few times. I haven't called her back.''

She sounded amazed. ''You didn't like her?''

He grinned. ''Not especially. I like you a lot better. You have blue eyes.''

''So does my cousin Cindy,'' she said quickly. ''I could introduce you to her.''

He jerked erect and strode out of the water, stopping just inches from her. He wanted to drag her into his arms and show her how interested he was in her cousin, who by all accounts sounded as flighty and shallow, as Mary Evans was predatory.

She backed away, her eyes filled with alarm. That annoyed him almost as much as her offering to find someone else for him.

''Why would I want to meet your cousin Cindy?'' he asked, making no attempt to disguise his impatience. ''I've already met you.'' He looped a hand behind her neck, sliding it under the wet heaviness of her ponytail. "What makes you think you're not enough to keep me occupied for the duration of my vacation? A guy can have more than one vacation project at a time you know."

"But Cindy... She's fun. She's cute. She's full of life."

He swept his gaze over her, lingering just long enough so he could be sure she realized it, on her erect nipples showing through her swimsuit. "And you're dead?"

She pulled her towel tightly across her front, lapping it over, hiding herself from him. "Compared to her, I might as well be. I'm not as...interesting as she is."

She drew a deep breath and let it out in a whoosh. "Look, I've thought about this a lot, Keith. You've led a much more...exciting life than I have. I imagine you've known lots of really sophisticated women. I don't think I'm quite in your class, and I'd appreciate it if you'd quit trying to seduce me just because you're a bit bored and lonely."

"What if I were to say I wasn't trying to seduce you because I'm bored?"

"I wouldn't believe you." He watched her throat work as she swallowed. Her face paled. "I'm not interested in a vacation fling. I had one once, and it caused me all sorts of heartache. The very thought of doing it again terrifies me. It scares me nearly as much as setting off on a world tour. But since I think the tour would be more educational, I plan to overcome my fears and do just that, so I won't have time for anything else, even if I wanted it."

If she wanted it? Keith thought. *Oh, she wanted it all right, as badly as he did.* Maybe she wasn't ready to admit it yet, not even to herself, but he knew the truth.

He remembered the way her mouth had trembled apart under his that very first morning they met when he'd obeyed the impulse to kiss her, the way her body had quivered in his arms. He remembered the way her lip had stroked his finger when he fed her that raspberry.

Snapping back to the matter at hand, he said, "World tour? Last I heard, it was just the Galápagos Islands."

"Maybe I should consider expanding my horizons," she said, but he saw the way her gaze swept over him, and read in her eyes the same kind of hunger she elicited in him. She wanted to expand her horizons in exactly the same direction he did, but she was scared.

All right. Maybe it was time to fish or cut bait—and make her do the same.

"I'm attracted to you, Ali. I want to—" He couldn't tell her what he wanted to do. Not yet. "I want to get to know you better."

Again, he saw temptation in her face, but heard anxiety along with suspicion in her voice. "How well?"

"As a...as a good friend," he said. "All I really know about you is that you pretend to be placid, but you throw dishes. You pretend to be a creature of routine, but you're willing to break that routine to baby-sit for a neighbor at a moment's notice. You interest me, you constantly surprise me and didn't you admit you wanted to be in my arms?"

She puffed out another sharp breath. "I did not! I admitted I wanted to be in that store, and you know it!"

He drew her closer and brushed his mouth over hers. "I also like to kiss you because it makes your eyes look bluer."

"How can it?" she scoffed. "Blue is blue. It doesn't change."

He grinned. "Ah, but when I kiss you, you blush and the contrast with your pink cheeks makes your eyes bright." He did it again, just as lightly, just as quickly, and then laid the back of his hand against her cheek. "There, can you feel the heat? I can see it."

Her breathing was rapid and a pulse all but rattled in her throat. "I wish you'd quit doing that," she said, her voice ragged. "You said you wouldn't try to seduce me."

He laughed. "And I wish you'd quit fibbing, but I won't kiss you again without your permission on one condition."

She looked wary, but he sensed that simmering excitement she never seemed quite able to suppress. "And what would that be?"

"You help me with my vacation project."

Her eyes widened and he hastened to say, "Renovating that boat, Ali!"

"Oh." Did he detect a hint of disappointment in her face and tone? He was sure of it, and it produced more than just a smidgen of simmering excitement in him.

"I don't know the first thing about renovating a boat," she protested.

"I do," he replied easily, sinking onto a beached log and patting the space beside him. "Sit down and I'll tell you all about *Tadpole* and what we'll be doing to her."

Because she couldn't think of a valid reason not to, Ali accepted his invitation, though not quite as close to him as his patting hand had indicated.

Ninety percent of the confidence she thought she'd learned in class had deserted her the minute he'd wrapped his hand around the back of her neck. His touch did that so easily, as easily as any of those smoldering looks he could bestow, as swiftly as one of his softly spoken compliments could undo all her pretense of feeling positive about herself.

It was a paradox. When he said something nice to her, instead of making her feel good about herself, it made her feel nervous, as if maybe his aunt had told him how utterly dateless she was, and he was trying to be kind. Except the expression in his eyes after he kissed her wasn't that of a man just trying to be kind. He looked like a man enjoying himself.

And her. It was a novel experience. Maybe, to him, she really was exciting?

"Our family has had this boat since the summer I was nine and my brother, Dan, ten. We learned to sail right out there," he said with a gesture at the bay Ali had just swum across.

"After we were competent enough to be turned loose, we spent many summer hours being everything from pirates, Huck Finns, and shipwrecked mariners, to intrepid voyagers discovering new lands. Those, we claimed in the name of the kingdom of Keithdania."

He grinned. "At least, I called it Keithdania. Dan called it Dankeithia on the days when it was his turn to be captain."

"That sounds fair. What did you intrepid voyagers do, go around planting flags on uninhabited spots along the lakeshore?"

"I, uh, well—" He chuckled, a low, warm sound that made her tingle deep inside. "Promise you won't tell Aunt Ruth? I'm serious about this. Cross your heart."

Mystified but entertained, Ali complied.

"We didn't plant flags, exactly," he whispered. "We, uh, staked our territory, uh, differently."

She leaned closer to hear him better. "Well? How?"

"You ever seen a male dog staking out his territory?"

"Oh, you didn't!" she laughed.

He nodded. "We did. Trouble was, we weren't always careful to ensure our newly discovered lands didn't have previous inhabitants. We were having a contest one day to see who'd get to claim the largest circle on one particular headland when the lady who'd gotten there first jumped up from behind the shelter of a log where she'd been sunbathing in the raw. I can only say she wasn't pleased with what we'd done to her hairdo.

"That was the day I learned I could run faster than my brother."

When Ali finished laughing, she said, "I don't believe you. You made that up. What are you, a novelist or something?"

He shrugged, glancing away from her. "Something." His tone was flat. "I'm a photojournalist."

She sobered. "Your aunt said you'd spent the last half of your life wandering around different war zones. Isn't that very dangerous?"

He stood abruptly, returning to the boat. "Sometimes." He bent and rapped on the hull with his kuckles. "She probably hasn't been in the water for fifteen years. She'll need to soak for a few days."

Ali feigned astonishment. "Your aunt Ruth?"

He grinned as he waded ashore. *"Tadpole,"* he said, ruffling her frizzy, half-dried bangs with a wet hand as if she were a ten-year-old. "Aunt Ruth probably hasn't been in the water for sixty years," he added, and they both grinned.

It was nice, Ali decided, sharing small, silly moments with him. Obviously he didn't want to talk about his life away from this place, but maybe he would once they knew each other better.

"So how do we go about this renovation task? A bit of sanding, some slaps of paint and we're done?" To her, that sounded good for maybe an afternoon.

He shook his head as he resumed his seat on the log. Red lights glinted in the dark strands of his hair. "She'll need a lot more than paint. Scraping and caulking and patching. We may have to replace some planks. Then will come the sanding and painting, followed by sanding and painting again. Likely a new mast, and definitely a new sail, to say nothing of new gear and rigging, all of which has to be installed. By us, before we even give her a sea-trial."

He launched into a detailed explanation of different types of sailing rigs, then segued into his plans for refurbishing *Tadpole.*

Ali listened fascinated, and watched as he bent forward and drew diagrams in the sand with a forefinger. She wasn't bored any longer. Nor was she lonely. She had, she realized, been lonely for much of her life, even when she was married to Leo. Maybe especially then.

At length, Keith stopped and gazed guiltily at her. "Good Lord! You're still awake?"

She couldn't hold in the happy laugh that bubbled forth. "You hoped to put me to sleep?"

His eyes showed a rueful smile. "I could have, going on like that."

"I don't remember so much as a single yawn."

"Only because you're a very polite woman. Do you like sailing?"

Ali shrugged. "That remains to be seen. I've never even been aboard a boat smaller than a car-ferry, but I'd like to try it."

Without really meaning to, she told him about Cindy's moonlight sail while he listened with the same kind of attentiveness he'd shown that first day. As before, it encouraged her to say more than she intended. "I probably wouldn't have enjoyed it much," she concluded. "When Cindy and her friends get together, they play their music so loud it makes my head ache."

"When we get *Tadpole* shipshape, we'll go out for a moonlight sail together. And there won't be any loud music. Just you and me and the swish of water on the hull." He lowered his voice. "And maybe then we'll go for a moonlight swim."

It took Ali a minute to fight off the delicious tremors his words sent through her. "I'm probably not brave enough for moonlight swims."

"Sure you are," he chided. "I mean, a woman who plans a trip to the Galápagos has to have lots of courage."

She sighed. "I'm not sure I'm brave enough for that, either."

It might take several more sessions with Katerina Boyd to get her self-confidence up to standard.

"Maybe...maybe you could teach me a bit about foreign travel and...things? Just to give me a few pointers about how to survive in strange situations?"

Keith smiled that sleepy, sexy smile of his and ran a curved finger down her face from temple to chin. "Honey, by the time I get through teaching you all the things you need to learn, you'll be brave enough for anything."

Ali swallowed hard and glanced away from his half-shuttered eyes. Her breath caught and her heart stalled. She didn't think for a minute he'd been talking about offering her travel tips. She edged away, crossing her arms over herself. He *was* trying to seduce her. Maybe he just couldn't help himself. Maybe it was in his nature to seduce any woman he met.

She wondered how he'd feel if the tables were turned, if a woman tried to seduce him. But then, it sounded as if Mary Evans already had, and he hadn't liked it. He'd called Mary predatory. But he'd also said she, Ali, surprised him. Wouldn't it surprise him if she tried to seduce him?

She felt her face burn and knew the thought had brought forth another bright blush.

Suddenly Keith shot to his feet and said, "You've been out in the sun too long. Come on, it's time I got you into the shade before you burn to a crisp. Lesson number one in foreign travel, Ali. Always wear a hat in sunny climes."

The minute Keith drew Ali to her feet, her hand

locked warm and tight in his made her body yearn to be locked warm and tight in his arms. Thinking of that made her shiver despite the warmth of the sun. He was seducing her without even trying. Maybe without even knowing, and that thought made her sad.

They ate breakfast together at her house, then after she'd dutifully put on a hat, went back to the boat. When he offered her his T-shirt to put on over her bathing suit so her back wouldn't burn, she accepted. She wanted to hug its soft fabric to her and take it home with her, keep it forever, wear it to bed every night; having even so small a part of him as her own would make the time when he was gone more bearable.

But right now, she wouldn't think of that. Right now, she'd enjoy the moments, the days, she would be spending with him.

She'd enjoy them to the fullest.

HOW HAVING EVERY ONE of her nails broken down to jagged stubs, and having the skin worn off her knuckles and fingertips could be fun, Ali didn't know. But it was. As was getting sunburned and dirty and more tired than she'd ever been in her life before each day was done. But she'd certainly been sleeping well, and waking eager for the next day to begin all week long.

She'd taken one afternoon off to attend her second seminar, and had begun to feel much more comfortable inside her own skin. She'd even begun to think that maybe Keith really did like her for herself, though he'd more or less quit trying to seduce her. Sometimes, she missed that.

No, Katerina had said "never lie to yourself." If she was to be truthful, she had missed his seductive behavior every day, his quick, impulsive kisses, but true to his promise not to kiss her again unless she said he should, he hadn't. She'd missed that, too.

Maybe that was why she'd ended up with that ridiculous number five goal on her list. The first time it had occurred to her, she was in a bit of a temper and had meant it as a joke, yet it kept popping into her mind so often, she finally put it on the list. In writing, it looked even more terrifyingly daring.

She was just glad no one but she would ever see it.

"Have some more potato salad, Alison," Mrs. Rathbury said, passing Ali the bowl. With Ali and Keith so busy on the boat, Mrs. Rathbury was doing nearly all the cooking.

"Thanks, I've had plenty, and I have a one-o'clock appointment in Kentonville," she said, "but I should be finished before the stores close. Is there anything we need from the building supply, Keith?"

"I don't think so," he said. Then, walking her home, one arm draped companionably over her shoulders, he asked, "How long do you think you'll be?"

"I should be finished my cla—my appointment by four or four-thirty," she said, "then I'll get a few groceries and...things, and be home by about five-thirty."

Keith turned her face up. "Buying groceries makes you blush?"

Her face grew hotter. "Ah, I see," he said. "It's not so much the groceries, as the 'things.' Right?"

If only he knew! Not that she probably would buy those "things," but if number five was the one she ultimately chose, then she figured she'd need them.

Quickly Ali said, "Will the last coat of paint be dry enough for a sanding by the time I get back?"

He shrugged. "Even if it is, it can wait till morning. Let's take the evening off. I think by then I'll have something important I want to discuss with you. How does dinner sound?"

To Ali, it sounded like heaven. Until he said, "Give me fifteen minutes to shower and put on some clean clothes and I'll drive in with you. I have an appointment in K'ville, too, this afternoon. No point in taking two cars. Then we can shop together."

"No!" she all but squealed. No way was she going to have him discover she was taking the third in the series of assertiveness training seminars. Especially this one. She'd need all the time it took to drive home alone to come to terms with whichever goal she finally decided on. Especially if it was number five.

Which she was sure it would be.

Today's seminar was the one where they had to discuss the lists they'd each been working on, lists of five things they wanted to do, needed to do for their own personal growth, but were afraid to do.

Katerina had said last week that today would be the moment of truth. They would each have to decide. Luckily they didn't have to tell which one they'd chosen to attack, but the following week, they'd have to say if they'd done it, and how the result had made them feel.

Her list was now neatly written in her notebook under the heading of Things To Do To Achieve Personal Growth, and each time she thought of the number five item on it, she blushed. "I...I have to leave right now or I'll be late."

Keith stroked his fingers over her hot face, raised his brows, but shrugged. "Okay, then, how about I meet you outside the supermarket about four forty-five and we'll take it from there?"

That, she could live with. At least she'd have her own car.

BY THE TIME ALI ARRIVED in Kentonville, she had convinced herself that number five on her list was too big a step for her to take. She'd probably choose number one, or maybe number four. Nobody ever said she had to start big.

Before they got to the list part in the seminar, each of them had participated willingly and eagerly and successfully in acting out some of the scenarios Katerina set up between participants.

Job interviews, with each of them taking a turn at being interviewee and interviewer. Returning an unsatisfactory purchase to a store. Facing down an agressive co-worker whose ideas clashed with her own. Lessening the possibility of date-rape by saying no in an unmistakable decisive manner.

They ran a fun exercise, giving themselves nicknames they felt could epitomize their newly developing characters. There was Brenda the Bold, Sylvia the Sure, Kathy the Competent, Andrea the Able. Ali would have liked that one herself, and had to think long and hard, rejecting several as not producing the image she really wanted. When one of the others, trying to help, laughingly suggested "Ali the Hun," she knew it was exactly right.

Then the moment had arrived. "Take out your lists now. Look them over one more time, and check the one you mean to accomplish over the next week."

Ali the librarian looked at her list, which had been written and rewritten so many times it scarcely bore resemblance to the original one.

1. Tell Cindy no more free dressmaking.
2. Let Mary Evans know I don't appreciate her sons stealing raspberries and cucumbers.
3. Learn how to drive a standard shift car so I can rent a Jeep and go exploring in the Andes or some other mountainous country.

4. Tell my mother to quit buying trousseau items for a daughter destined never to marry again.
5. Seduce Keith Devon so I'll have a great memory to take with me on trips, and maybe some experience I can use if the occasion ever arises again.

Ali the librarian scanned the list twice, three times, glanced around the room, saw other women busily and confidently making tick marks on theirs.

She put her pen against number one, the easiest, then frowned. The Evans boys were becoming a distinct nuisance, but she also hated to see her mother waste good money on clothing Ali kept hidden in a bottom drawer and never, ever wore.

It was very hard to decide. She wasn't sure she had the necessary coordination to learn to drive a standard shift vehicle.

She looked at it again, and heard a laughing voice in her head say, "Ali the Hun, are you a total wimp?"

Before she could change her mind, she made a big, bold check mark against number five.

And then she blushed so hard she thought the off-white walls must surely be reflecting her pink glow.

She slapped her notebook closed and sat listening half attentively to Katerina's saying that next week, they'd get into public speaking.

Though this news was met with groans Ali joined, she felt her heartbeat accelerate as she began to plan what she'd say and how she'd say it. Learning how to be assertive was fun, as well as good for her. And if she could accomplish number five, maybe that was what she'd use as the subject of her speech.

The thought not only made her blush furiously again, but it also made her laugh.

Ali the Hun. She laughed to herself all the way to the drugstore, and then to the supermarket.

She picked up a few items there, remembering to make eye contact and smile at the man behind the till as she paid for her purchases, as she had not been able to do in the drugstore. She visited the bank machine near the corner, then, still half-dazed by her sense of self-discovery, crossed at the light.

In the middle of the intersection, she stopped for a moment and smiled as inspiration struck.

With her newfound sense of self-confidence, she could probably even bring herself to advertise for a traveling companion, thereby overcoming the problem the travel agent had explained, about the single-occupancy surcharge.

Unbidden, the image of Keith's dark hair and tan face rose in her mind, and her heart flipped over a time or two. *Stop it,* she told herself sternly. *Adventure is one thing, but traveling with a man like him would be downright foolhardy. He'd probably take me to one of his war zones or something.*

Foolhardy or not, the notion held considerable appeal. She certainly wouldn't have to bother with a tour group of total strangers, or a roommate she didn't know.

Then she imagined herself and a thoroughly seduced Keith walking hand in hand along the side of a romantic canal in Venice, or drifting in the moonlight while a gondolier sang a love song to them.

Keith would draw her into his arms the way he had that first day they'd met, only this time she wouldn't be weeping from shock and loss. This time she'd be a willing, eager participant, the way she'd been for that shocking moment in the doorway to the Glass House.

She'd lift her face to his and, instead of jerking away as she had then, she'd wait while he lowered his head and kissed her. She'd kiss him back, tasting his musk, and melt into his embrace, oblivious of her surroundings.

That wouldn't matter, of course, because gondoliers were used to that. They expected it.

And Keith—oh, he'd expect a lot from a woman. From *his* woman. When the gondola arrived back at their hotel, he'd lift her in his arms, carry her inside past a startled desk clerk and up a sconce-lit curving flight of stairs such as she'd seen in an old, black-and-white movie set in Venice.

In their room, moonlight would flood through

the open windows. Soft, warm breezes would waft over them as he tenderly slid her black silk teddy from her body and...

She continued on, lost in the pleasure of her fantasy as she reached her car and unlocked the trunk. She set down the grocery bag, and tenderly slid her notebook inside it. Her precious notebook stuffed with information on how she could make herself over into the kind of woman a man like Keith Devon would be delighted to travel with, thrilled to be seduced by.

Absentmindedly she pulled the keys from the lock. As she put her hand on the lid of the trunk to push it down, she was swept off her feet.

7

ONE MINUTE ALI was standing beside her car, and the next she was scooped up, shoved into the trunk with her groceries. The lid slammed, cutting off the light and her startled, protesting yelp.

She flexed her right hand, her fingers sore and aching. Whoever had attacked her, had snatched her keys right out of her hand! Doors slammed. The engine roared to life. The car lurched forward. There came the screech of brakes and she braced herself for impact, but none came.

The car swayed sharply as it was flung around a corner, jerked the other way as it turned again. It bumped over railroad tracks, rumbled along a dirt road, bouncing in and out of potholes.

Had her abduction been witnessed? Had anyone called the police? She tried to rememeber if there had been any passersby on the street, but couldn't recall seeing a soul.

She listened for sirens, prayed for sirens, but none sounded.

She heard, over the thunder of the wheels on the gravel road, a loud triumphant yell: "Ya-hoo!" and braying, male laughter.

Oh, God help her! There were two of them! At

least two, and they were cheering about their act! Obviously they, too, were just as aware as she was of the lack of pursuit.

Determined not to cry from sheer terror, Ali recited to herself as many as she could recall of the uplifting thoughts she had gleaned from her last seminar.

"You can only be made a victim by your own choice."

"Let me go!" she yelled. "Keep the car. Keep the money! Just let me go!"

If they heard her, there was no indication. The radio switched from her favorite classic rock station to one blaring out hard rock.

She needed to think, to reason things out. What could be their purpose? The deadly combination of the car's rattling over the rough road and the blaring radio made rational thought almost impossible.

Another jolt and she bit her tongue, tasting the acrid flavor of her own blood.

She gagged. Was she about to be murdered? Her whole body shook. Why had she been kidnapped? What did they want with her? Oh, God, was this her punishment for thinking she deserved a bit of adventure in her life? If this was adventure, she hated it!

She was scared, hurt, bruised and battered from the unyielding floor of the trunk as the car continued to lurch along, still at an alarmingly high rate of speed. The volume from the rear speakers was hurting her ears and making her dizzy.

She gulped air too fast, knew she was hyperventilating, but when she tried to stop, an overwhelming sense of suffocation forced her to gasp deeply, rapidly again and again, escalating the lightheadedness.

What would Katerina do in a situation like this?

For one thing, she wouldn't panic. She'd get herself in a position to fight. Katerina wouldn't just lie around waiting for someone else to save her. She'd do something, something...assertive. And so must Ali. It was that, or be prepared to forfeit her life when they stopped and opened the trunk.

Wait. She'd read a book where someone was dumped in the trunk of a car. A detective. What had he done? She had only to remember. The answer to all the questions in the world could be found in books. She squeezed her eyes shut and forced herself to think.

Yes. The tire iron. He'd held it under him, pretending to be unconscious when the crooks stopped the car and opened the trunk. When one of them had rolled him over, he'd flown up, flailing with the implement and bashed both of them over the head. He'd gotten away.

Odd, how in picturing that scene, she saw Keith as the man who had foiled the crooks....

Keith! She had just met a man who fascinated her, appealed to her like no other ever had and she was damned if she was going to let her life get snuffed out the minute it got interesting.

Now, where was her tire iron?

Oh, yeah. Right.

Her tire iron was in a little hatch underneath the bottom of the trunk along with the spare tire, and she was lying on that hatch. However she wriggled and changed positions, there was no way she could get at it unless she first got out of the trunk.

A series of sharp turns made the car jolt like crazy. Her grocery bag tipped over, spilling fresh fruits and vegetables all around her. She wished she'd bought something hard and heavy, like a can of pumpkin she could use as a club. Maybe she could bean one of them with her cantaloupe, but there'd still be the other one to deal with. Besides, she didn't think a ripe cantaloupe was likely to be lethal. All she'd do is make the guy mad.

She bounced up right off the trunk floor and came down hard, mashing a tomato under her right breast.

The loud rock music continued to assault her.

Ali wrapped her arms around her head and cried.

Another bump lifted her, thumped her against the inside of the trunk lid and flopped her back onto the floor. Another tomato smashed under her temple.

Feeling sick, she smeared it from her eye, but it clung to her hands, to her clothes, her face, spread into her hair, and was surely ruining the gray carpet of the trunk.

She realized it was also soaking into her notebook.

She strugged to pull the book out from under

her, and succeeded only in tearing its now soggy pages.

"Dammit, I need that material!"

Suddenly debilitating fear gave way to a sweep of fury at the indignity that had been imposed on her. They were ruining her notebook!

"Who the hell do you think you kidnapped?" she yelled at her unhearing assailants. "You thought you had some timid little librarian locked up in here, didn't you? Well, have I got news for you! What you have in this trunk is *Ali the Hun!*"

Saying it made her feel better. Saying it again, louder, gave her greater confidence, especially since she knew they couldn't hear her over the heavy metal tune playing on the radio. Squirming around, she continued to search for something, anything, that could be used as a weapon. One foot struck the back of the back seat, and a glimmer of light entered the trunk.

Ali went motionless.

Oh, my gosh! Yes! Of course!

Her car was built so sections of the seat back would fold forward to facilitate a load too long for the trunk. On the left, a narrow flap, on the right, a wide one. Opened together, they were plenty big enough to permit her escape.

That was her way out! Once in the back seat, she'd fling open a door, roll out and...and they were traveling at a rate of speed that would make such an action as deadly as her abductors likely were.

So, what if she waited until they stopped? While they were coming around to open the trunk, she'd slide into the front of the car, hit the master lock and be safe from them. Except—they'd have the keys. If she sneaked out of the car without their noticing, they could still come after her and finish her off with no trouble at all.

So, jumping out at high speeds was impractical. Staying in the car until they left was also impractical. They might not leave! For another thing, she didn't have a clue where they might be taking her. When they stopped, would they be at some kind of a crooks' hideout? A drug-runners' enclave? There could be dozens of armed desperadoes surrounding the car.

Oh, Lord! Was she about to be bundled into a small airplane and flown to South America and held as a hostage—or worse! Didn't the Fates understand that this was absolutely not what she'd had in mind when it came to foreign travel? She hadn't even had a chance to research South America properly. That was supposed to have come next.

Next? Was she going to have a chance at anything remotely resembling "next" unless it was a bullet in her head?

Dammit, that kind of thinking was defeatist. Was she going to lie down and let some desperadoes kill her without putting up a fight?

No! She was getting out of this mess, and not feetfirst.

If she popped out of the trunk into the back seat

suddenly enough, she'd take them by surprise. What she'd do then, she had no idea, but she did know that she wasn't going to lie curled up in the trunk of the car, crying, until they decided to let her out.

It was going to be *her* way from here on in.

"Take the initiave," Katerina had said. "Become *pro*active, not *re*active. Your life, your happiness, your needs are your business. No one cares about you more than you."

Well, for sure she cared about herself more now than she'd cared in the past. Katerina had seen to that.

And so had Keith.

That thought popped out of nowhere, but she knew it was true. If she let these goons snuff out her life before it had properly begun, she'd never get a chance to learn all those lessons Keith had promised to teach her—especially the ones his eyes had promised, but he had yet to make good on.

Those were the ones she most wanted.

Katerina Boyd's lessons might turn her into a confident, effectual human being.

Keith's would turn her into the woman she had always secretly wanted to be. Complete with whipped cream!

If she lived long enough.

Her eyes adjusted slowly in the faint light seeping in through the seat back, finally allowing her to see a few inches around her. She managed to turn herself, getting up on her hands and knees, head facing the front of the car. She lost plenty of skin and heard her skirt rip up one seam, but as she groped for good purchase from which to launch her attack, her hand encountered a...a weapon.

Yes. This, and surprise, might just be the difference between success and failure.

With her "weapon" in her fist, she positioned herself, bent her head and gave the seat back an almighty shove, sending both sections slamming forward.

In the same motion, she lunged through the gap, rolled to the right and jammed her weapon against the neck of the startled passenger.

"She's got a gun!" he screamed, freezing in terror as she'd hoped he would.

He stared with round blue eyes, head half turned toward the left, mouth open in a now wordless plea to the driver, who spared Ali only the briefest glance. She realized they were both boys, probably not even fifteen, and undoubtly the driver was unlicensed. At the speed they were traveling, she was glad he kept his eyes on the road.

Praying he'd continue to do so, and that the passenger would continue to keep his face turned away from her weapon, she said, "Stop the car or I shoot your buddy right here," then added in a voice she thought Katerina Boyd would have been proud to own. "If I have to shoot him, you're next."

The car jerked around a tight bend, and swerved as the driver braked and fought to bring it back. He overcorrected, sending it rocketing in the other direction. Several trees loomed in front of the windshield for an instant, then a space opened and the car aimed for it.

"Look out!" the passenger screamed as the car left the dirt road and barreled along a ditch. It wobbled from side to side like a guttered bowling ball, slowing and grinding into the sandy soil before coming to rest in the bed of a creek, nose down at a forty-five degree angle.

To Ali, it all happened in slow motion, watching both front seat passengers flop forward, hearing their heads make hollow thuds, one against the padded plastic of the dash, the other against the steering wheel, and watching the windshield pop out, amazingly all in one piece to lie across the hood. It rocked there for a second, then slid off over the front.

The driver's long dark hair parted, revealing a dirty neck.

She scrambled from the car, and saw that the trunk had popped open. She snatched up her notebook, knowing only that she had to save it. She was about to run, to hide, to put as much distance between herself and the two in the front of her car as possible, when one of them groaned.

They were waking up. She had no time to flee!

She whirled in time to see the driver lift his head.

"Don't even think of moving," she said with authority that startled her.

"Don't shoot, lady!" he pleaded as he gripped

the wheel, his arms rigid, his eyes staring straight ahead. "Don't shoot."

To her amazement, sirens sang in the distance, growing closer, closer, but before any police cars arrived on the scene, a bronze Bronco slewed to a sudden stop not five feet from where Ali stood trembling.

She looked at the ashen-faced driver, saw his door fly open and tried to speak. No words came out.

All she could do was clutch her notebook to her chest and stare at Keith, wondering what in the world he was doing there.

Keith caught her in his arms, sick with relief that she was alive, whole, warm if trembling, but there, beside him, not being stolen away.

"Ali, my God, Ali, are you all right? Talk to me!" he groaned, patting her all over, desperately needing to touch her. He smoothed back her damp, smeared hair, and ran his fingers over her face, her red-stained blouse. "Oh, cripes, you're bleeding." How could he have come so close to losing her the very day he finally figured out a way of keeping her?

"No, I'm not," she said firmly. "Ali the Hun doesn't bleed. She—"

"Ali the *what?*" The sirens stopped and both police cars burst open, spilling out Mounties. The boy behind the wheel of Ali's car leaped out and took a flying lunge across the creek, heading for a thick stand of trees a hundred feet away.

Keith's loud and authorative "Hold it!" froze the kid in his tracks, and he stood, hands aloft, visibly shaking.

"Don't shoot," he said again, in a high, cracking voice.

Ali strode toward the ditch as the other kid alighted from the car and made a move to join his cohort. Without so much as a glance at Keith or the policemen, as if they didn't exist, she extended her arm and yelled, "Stop! Stop or I'll shoot!"

As if he had already been shot, the blond boy collapsed on the side of the creek bed, arms wrapped protectively around his head, while the other one jerked even stiffer.

"Ali!" Keith roared, trying to put himself between her and the boys.

"Get out of my way," she snarled. "You're in my line of fire."

"Line of—" He gaped at her. Cripes! She'd winged right out! Shock! He'd seen this before. She'd been through hell. Her eyes were wild, her clothing filthy, her hair all over, and her skin so white her freckles looked like rust spots on an enamel sink. *Ali the Hun?* Who the hell was she trying to kid?

"You're under arrest, mister," said the boss cop, drawing his gun and aiming it at Keith. "Now move carefully away from the lady."

Keith whirled. "Me? I'm under arrest? What the hell for?"

At the same time, the kid on the far side of the

ditch, his shaking hands still reaching high, quavered, "Make her put the gun away! Don't let her shoot me! I didn't mean it! It was him—Josh. He wanted to do it. Not me. I didn't. Oh, my God, my dad's gonna kill me!"

"O...kay," said one of the officers. "Suppose someone tells us exactly what is going on here? And lady, would you please put down that banana? You're scaring the kids."

Keith's "Scaring the *kids?*" blended with the voice of the boy on the high ground as he whirled. "*Banana?*"

The youth stared at Ali, at her "weapon," and took a couple of tentative steps toward the shelter of the woods. He thought better of it as another officer drew a gun that looked considerably more deadly than Ali's weapon.

Into the silence came the voice of the police dispatcher over the car radio: "...suspects are Caucasian male juveniles between the ages of thirteen and eighteen, one approximately five feet ten inches tall, one hundred sixty pounds, wearing jeans and a blue-and-white nylon jacket."

Ali's gaze pinned on the former passenger who bit his lip and closed his eyes, muttering something about his mom. Tears squeezed from between his lids, rolling down his cheeks. Ali felt sorry for him.

"The other is reported to be wearing a black T-shirt with black jeans. He is about six feet, and has a tattoo on his right forearm. Both wore ski masks and are wanted in connection with a convenience store robbery. They are to be considered armed and dangerous.''

As the cops collared both kids, Ali flung her arms around Keith, jubilation sending her off into raptures of joy.

''I did it! I did it!'' she shouted, hanging on to him and dancing around in a circle he had to follow or be tipped over. ''I tricked them! I proved myself. I told them to stop or I'd shoot and they stopped. They did, Keith! They believed me! They thought I was tough! I can do anything after this. I can go to Ecuador. I can go to Antarctica! I could make my way through your stupid war zones and look after myself! I can seduce you if I want to!''

Keith forced her to a halt. He gave her a small shake. ''Protect yourself? Look after yourself? Shoot the bad guys, Ali? With a *banana?*'' Seduce him? Had she said that, or was he going as crazy as she was?

Hell, of course he was going crazy. He'd had a bad shock, too, never a worse one than when he'd seen her scooped up and dumped into the trunk of her own car.

She looked down at the half-mashed fruit in her hand, at the tomato juice and pulp staining her clothing, at the boys being bundled into the back seats of two separate police cars. She looked at the wreck of her own car, crumpled nose buried in a rippling creek.

With a soft little moan, ''Ali the Hun'' passed out.

Keith caught her as she went down.

ALI CAME TO almost at once, as Keith slid her onto the passenger seat of his Bronco. He was silent, glum, dark-eyed with anger as he followed the police cars back to town.

He didn't even laugh or so much as crack a smile when, after they'd given their statements, the cops had started speculating on the headlines they'd read in the next day's papers: Banana Brandishing Babe Bags Boys. Another came in with Fruit Foils Felons, followed by Librarian Books Bandits. The suggestions deteriorated from there.

Keith just simmered and stared at the speeding ticket he'd been issued. No matter that they'd caught a couple of snatch-and-grab artists, no matter that they'd caught a pair of kidnappers and car thieves thanks to him. No matter that they wouldn't have been able to do any of that if they hadn't seen him in hot pursuit. Dammit, they still gave him a speeding ticket! *Cops!*

He was thundercloud quiet for the first few minutes as the reporters, from both print and electronic media set upon them as they left the police station. They'd be there, one of the officers had warned Ali. They all had police scanners, and kept abreast of matters that way.

Three different people plied Ali with questions: *What had gone through her mind the minute she was swept off her feet?*

"I thought it was Keith," she blurted, then could

have bitten out her tongue. She flashed him a guilty look as the reporter asked if he often stuffed women into the trunks of cars.

Keith just growled something only half intelligible about the lady being out of her head with shock.

What made her think she could save herself by pointing a banana at the perpetrators? All she could say to that was, "It was all I had."

She had worked at the Mitikiltuk library, hadn't she? Did she think there was any connection between her kidnapping and the suspected arson fire at the library? Could it be a personal vendetta against her for some reason?

Ali giggled at the suggestion. "What reason? Charging a fine for an overdue book?"

The cameraman snickered aloud.

What did she plan for her next act?

Oddly that made her mad. "What I did wasn't any kind of an act! Except maybe an act of desperation, borne of a strong desire to live." She raised her chin and went on, "But if you mean do I have plans, then yes, I do. They involve many more adventures, but ones of my own choosing."

She was now assertive enough to tell the truth about other things as well: "I've been attending assertiveness training seminars recently and I've accomplished a great deal of personal growth. Today, I think I've developed a taste for adventure. I feel I've proved myself capable of handling difficult and challenging situations and have no intention of going back.''

What kind of adventures? What did she see herself doing now that she was out of work? Had she applied at the Kentonville library? When she said ''not going back,'' did she think a job in another library would satisfy her new taste for adventure?

The questions came thick and fast and, while she was still on a roll, she decided to continue as long as her courage was up.

''World travel,'' she boasted, adrenaline high, pushing her to extremes. ''I'm going to explore every corner there is to be explored, and meet every danger and adventure head-on and with panache. I've renamed myself Ali the Hun and intend to make it stick.''

Keith stopped her by swinging her around and planting his mouth over hers. When he lifted it she was too stunned to say another word. She could do nothing but gape at him wondering what in the world had come over him, kissing her that way for no reason and in front of a TV camera.

''Ms. Kozinski has had more than enough adventure for one day,'' he said, ''and more than enough excitement. I'm taking her home now.''

''Are you Ms. Kozinski's boyfriend?''

''Of course not!'' Ali said, at the same moment as Keith snapped, ''That's Ms. Kozinski's and my private business.''

''If you're not involved, how come you went

chasing after her car instead of calling the police and letting them handle it?''

''There was no time to call—'' Keith began but one of the newspaper guys cut him off, pointing the end of a pen at Keith. ''Wait a minute! I recognize you. Keith Devon, *ActionBeat,* right? *That's* why you made the chase. You wanted to be in at the kill! Are you disappointed in the outcome? Will your magazine buy the story even though no one died? Will—''

Keith swung right from hip level and landed a solid blow on the reporter's chin. The man went down, the entire incident gleefully captured by a TV cameraman.

As if he didn't care, Keith all but dragged Ali away, stuffed her into his Bronco and burned rubber with the reporter climbing to his feet, shaking his head and the camera still grinding away.

''What's *ActionBeat?*'' she asked as they swept away down the street, heading for the highway.

''A magazine.'' He slammed on his brakes at the stop sign, then peeled out, turning right much too fast. He was up to highway speed in seconds. ''Nothing that would interest you.'' His tone warned her he didn't want to discuss it. Just as it had when he'd first mentioned he was a photojournalist.

Ali wasn't to be put off this time. ''What do you mean, it wouldn't interest me? I'm a librarian, for heaven's sake! I have—I had—a huge collection of periodicals but I don't recall seeing that one.''

"Not surprisingly," he snapped. "It would be completely out of place in a town like Mitikiltuk. Scare the pants off all the little old ladies, and turn the stomachs of even the strongest men."

"But you work for it? Going from war zone to war zone?"

"Yeah," he said. "Taking pictures and writing stories for a magazine specializing in action, adventure and excitement. Dead bodies, starving children, wailing, bereaved grandmothers."

"You don't sound happy about it."

He shrugged. "I'm not."

"Then why do you do it?"

"Now that," he said, "is one hell of a good question, one I've been asking myself over and over the past couple of weeks. I did it because at first it was exciting, challenging. Then I kept on doing it because it was all I knew how to do. All I thought I had. I suppose much in the same way it made sense to you attacking a couple of thugs with a goddamn banana!"

"I take it you pack a gun, in addition to a camera?"

"Yes."

His tone told her he chose not to pursue the subject, and he remained frustratingly silent all the rest of the way back to Mitikiltuk. If he was so ashamed of what he did, why didn't he quit? Ali thought.

Once home, he stomped into her kitchen and slammed her last bag of groceries onto the counter.

"There you were, wandering around with your

head in the clouds, not paying the least bit of attention to your surroundings."

Ali said nothing, only sipped the tea he had made for her even before carrying in the tumbled mess of junk he had rescued from the trunk of her car. He was appalled that she didn't have so much as a shot of brandy to lace the tea with.

"What do you normally do when you've had a shock?" he demanded.

"In Mitikiltuk? A shock? Like what, the newspaper coming ten minutes late?"

"Yeah, that," he agreed. "Or being kidnapped, or having your place of employment burn to the ground."

Feeling incredibly cocky, she laughed. "When I'm kidnapped, I point a banana at the crooks, then keel over when the danger's past. When my library burns down, I yell a lot and throw dishes, remember?"

He snorted, refusing to let her make light of the situation. "Dammit, Ali, you said you'd just left the bank machine. That, alone, should have made you cautious! *I* saw those kids running toward you. Even without having seen them yank off ski masks, *I'd* have known they were up to no good. If you haven't got the brains God gave a louse, how can you ever expect to be safe in really dangerous places?"

Ali wrapped her hands around her cup of steaming tea and slanted a suddenly wary glance at Keith.

He was seriously ticked off. And with her, not just the situation. He grabbed her tomato-stained notebook from the torn grocery bag, didn't look at it, only slapped it onto the table. She dragged it out from under his hand and tucked it beneath her arms.

Lord! What would he think if he saw her list, and saw that she'd selected number five? He thought she was a danger to herself now, he'd be even more sure of it if he saw that!

He was right, though. She had to acknowledge that much. Hearing two sets of running footsteps behind her, she should have at the very least turned and looked. But even then, would she have realized the crooks meant to steal her car?

"Apart from the ski masks, how could you tell they were up to no good?"

"Instinct," he said. "The way they moved, something about the set of their shoulders. It's intangible, but after a while, you learn to sense menace when it exists."

Of course he'd have learned that, working for a magazine that specialized in stories about dead bodies and wailing, bereaved grandmothers. Just thinking of it made her feel sick. What had actually seeing it done to him?

"But you," he went on, "you didn't even notice them coming." After a further smoldering look at her, Keith poured himself a cup of tea and topped up hers. He even stirred more sugar into it as if she was incapable of deciding how she liked her tea. Which was without any sugar at all!

Ali took his momentary inattention as an opportunity to reach over, and slide her notebook into the drawer in the side of the table.

"Anytime you hear running footsteps behind you, get ready to defend yourself," he lectured.

She stared at him. "Good grief! People jog, you know. I hear running footsteps all the time. What am I supposed to do, pack a pistol?"

As he did, when he was off on his dangerous magazine assignments. At the thought, which pointed out the basic differences between them, her spirits began to ebb, then to sink right to the bottom of the well as if someone had pulled a plug. He continued to glower across the table for a moment, then the faintest glimmer of a smile began in his eyes until it finally reached his mouth. "It would," he said, "beat the hell out of a banana."

Oddly, his smile, the easing of his anger, did nothing to lift her sagging mood. Now that he appeared to be over his need to rant, her ebullience deserted her.

Now that she no longer had a need to hold herself together to fight off his verbal onslaught, weariness overcame her, tearfulness, and a sickening realization of the truth. No matter how brave she thought she'd been, regardless of her exhilaration at having "triumphed" over the young thieves, she had accomplished nothing more than a very temporary standoff.

At any moment either of those kids would have seen what her "gun" really was, and her triumph would have been proven worthless. She had not rescued herself. Keith had rescued her. The cops had rescued her. Those boys had been considered "armed and dangerous."

She was not Ali the Hun. She was Ali the unemployed librarian. She was Predictable Polly and everyone was going to be jeering at her ridiculous, public boasts by this time tomorrow. She'd be the laughingstock of Mitikiltuk.

With a choking sound, she buried her head in her arms on the table and burst into tears.

"Ali!" She heard Keith's chair scrape across the floor, felt his hands on her as he came around to her side of the table. "Come on, honey, don't cry *now*. It's all over!"

She lifted her head. "I'm...not...cry-i-ing," she lied, but she could scarcely see him. The overhead light caught those shafts of red in the darkness of his hair; the tears in her eyes created a halo of spangled rubies around his head.

8

"OH, HELL, you are, too. You'll be okay. You're suffering a bit of delayed reaction."

He drew her out of her chair, holding her close, rocking her gently from side to side. Her brain told her to push him away, but her body burrowed close as her hands slid under his arms and around his back. He felt so good, so solid, so...secure.

"It's all over, Ali, you're safe now, and you did a great job today. You impressed me with your gutsy actions. You impressed the cops, and you sure as hell impressed those kids with your lethal banana."

"Then why have you been yelling at me ever since we got home? I don't want to be yelled at. I want to be...held. If this is how you treat all those poor, bereaved grandmothers, no wonder you're ashamed of what you do for a living!"

Keith stroked her tangled hair back from her face as he tucked her head beneath his chin, murmuring soft, silly things she loved to hear. Ali nestled against him. Dammit, what was she doing? Where was the spine she thought she'd developed as the result of her seminar sessions? It had about as much substance and strength as her knees.

"I had mascara all over my face. My hair was a mess. I'll be on television in a dirty slip! Everyone I know will see me, Mitikiltuk's ex-assistant head librarian, looking like a bag lady on the evening news!" she wept.

"You didn't look like a bag lady! You looked like you'd been thrown in the trunk of a car with some ripe tomatoes. Besides, you weren't being interviewed as the Librarian of the Year! You'd just heroically saved yourself after a terrifying experience. No one will expect you to look your best on TV."

"You just don't understand!" she wept. "I never go out of the house with dirty underwear!"

That it had been clean when she put it on held no meaning now. People had seen her with dirty underwear and she could almost hear her grandmother rotating, bony hips and shoulders knocking against the inside of her casket.

"I'm sorry," he said. "I shouldn't have yelled at you. It's just, well... Hell! Seeing those two goons stuff you into the trunk and take off, knowing my car was facing the wrong direction for fast pursuit, knowing I was in unfamiliar terrain and if I lost sight of them for a minute I might never find you again and..."

He tilted her face up and looked into her eyes. "Well, it scared the hell out of me."

Ali found her tears had stopped. Just a little bit of cuddling, and she felt whole again. "I didn't mean to scare you. I—" She broke off, frowning, before saying she was sorry. Hadn't Katerina told them not to apologize for things that weren't their fault?

"I was deep in thought," she said.

"What about?"

"You." The word popped out before she could stop it and she stared at him. "I mean, well... You know." She shrugged, tried to step away, but he held her, flattening her hand on his chest, smoothing his thumb gently over the backs of her fingers.

He regarded her, silent, thoughtful for a moment, then said softly, "No, I don't know, Ali. Can you be more specific? What were you thinking about me? You told those reporters you thought it was me who'd grabbed you. Why?"

Ali laughed, this time managing to break free of his hold. It was harder to break free of her desire to be held. Harder still not to tell him the truth. "I just said that...because," she said, aware of how high and false her voice sounded, "because I was, well, thinking about you. The way anyone would about a...friend they didn't know well and, well, maybe would like to know better and...I was thinking about gondolas, and Venice and moonlight and you—someone like you—I mean, sort of, well, sweeping me off my feet. It was a fantasy, for pity's sake. Fantasies don't mean anything."

"Venice, and gondolas, and moonlight...and me? Me, sweeping you off your feet?"

She sat and took a gulp of her now-cool tea,

staring at the table. "Just in a...general sense. You know."

"Do I?" His voice told her he'd moved closer. Did he understand how much she longed for his kisses, for more than the little tastes he'd given her of the passion she sensed could flare between them like a match in gasoline? If he did, he'd made no move she could recognize as striking a match.

"I'm not sure I do know, Ali," he said. "Why don't you tell me what other fantasies you have? About me."

"Not about you, specifically," she said, not entirely truthfully. He was so close his breath fluttered wisps of hair around her cheek. She grabbed it and bundled it at her nape, hoping it would stay there. Naturally, given its nature, it did not.

Keith slid one finger under it and tucked it behind her right ear. "But I do fantasize about doing some of the things Cindy does," she went on, her voice suddenly deeper than normal. "Like that moonlight sail...I've fantasized about that."

"I know. And I told you we'd do it." He tucked her hair behind her left ear, too, then slid his hand over it, as if trying to smooth its wildness. She knew it was a lost cause. "What else did Cindy do?" he asked.

Again, as he had since that very first day, he asked his questions in such a manner she found it impossible not to answer.

"She...went swimming. In the dark."

"Skinny-dipping?"

She jerked her head up and met his gaze. His face was bland, almost expressionless. "Well, actually, yes, she did, but that doesn't mean that I've fantasized about that, or I want to do it. With you. Or anyone else."

"Okay," he said. "Fair enough. What other fantasies, Ali?"

He waited patiently for her reply, and suddenly she realized what he was doing. He was *interviewing* her! Every time they'd had a conversation and he'd gotten her talking about things she never discussed with anyone, it wasn't because he cared, it was because that was what he was trained to do. That was how a journalist worked.

She gave him a smile that she hoped he'd see as blasé, one she thought might be Cindy-like. "Nope. Now it's your turn."

"Ali..." Suddenly his hands were on her shoulders. His eyes went darkly intense. "Don't play games with me."

Ali popped to her feet. "Don't play games with you?" She sucked in a deep breath. "Why not, Keith? Isn't that what this is all about? Isn't that what you were doing with me? Asking me questions you'd ask of a subject you wanted to write about? The way those reporters did tonight?"

His jaw squared off as his lips went so tight a white line formed between his nose and their corners. "No," he said. "That's not what I was doing when I was learning about you. I was doing it for myself, because I care about you, Ali. I want more than you think I want."

"What?" Her word was weak, her tone unsteady. "What is it you want?"

"I want you. And I don't want you to go away on any world travels."

She stared at him. *"Why?"*

"Ali..." Something in his tone stilled her heart. Something in his eyes made it jerk to erratic life again. She wished he wouldn't look at her that way, making her heartbeat stagger, putting an ache in her chest and heat deep in her belly.

She watched his eyes darken, saw a small muscle jump in his jaw just below his ear, heard his breathing in the utter silence of the room. She heard someone's heart beating. His, or hers?

She drew in a deep breath, aware of the sharp scent of lemon in the saucer by her tea, the sweet, heavy scent of honeysuckle on the fence, the tang of pine. The scent of Keith's skin. Never in her life had she been more aware of...anything than she was of her surroundings in this moment.

"Don't you think I have a few fantasies of my own?" he asked. "I spend most of every night, and all my days, fantasizing about you, vitally aware of you. I've been trying hard not to let you know that, not to bother you with it, but—"

He fell silent and shrugged.

Tensely she whispered, "Why?" again and saw his eyes darken almost to black. He continued to watch her. She continued to meet his steady, seeking gaze. She sensed he held his breath now as tightly as she held hers, as if breathing would break some kind of safety device that held them each in place.

"Because I—" He broke off. "Because I know what you want, dammit! You've made that eminently clear. You even went public with it today. Adventure! Travel! Challenges! You want to go out and see what the world is all about, on your own, and that thought scares the bejeezus out of me because I already know what it's all about and I know the perils you're going to face."

He pulled in a long breath. "I know you have a right to the life you've never had. A right to the excitement you've suddenly learned you crave. A right to—"

"A right to what?" she whispered, but he continued only to look at her silently.

"A right to do this?" She put her arms around his neck and moved in close. "A right to show you some of my fantasies? And to prove to you that I am not a Bambi?"

He caught her in his arms and cupped the back of her head in one hand. "Ali..." he said in a low, taut growl, then bent his head and took her mouth in the kind of kiss she'd been wanting since the minute she first saw him.

It was far more of a kiss than she'd anticipated. More of a kiss than she'd ever participated in. It started slow, but after a first, explorative tasting of each other, something huge and flamboyant flowered between them.

Her fingers locked around his shoulders, slid up over his neck, and he stroked his hands down her back, molding her to him.

As her lips parted, he accepted the invitation. Her tongue met his, thrust for generous thrust, tangling with his, as her fingers tangled in his hair.

He lifted his head, looked down at her. Ali licked her lips, thought she should say something, but all that emerged was a long, drawn-out, "Ohhh."

"Yeah," he breathed, cradling her close, pressing her cheek to his. He moved slightly, his beard stubble rasping her skin so erotically she shivered.

He ran a fingertip down her spine. A shudder coursed through her. He pulled her closer to him, tighter, his arms banding around her. She clung, a small sound escaping from her throat as he kissed her again, even more deeply.

Moments later, as Ali thought her knees were about to collapse, he lifted his mouth from hers and breathed her name across her cheek. She gasped for oxygen, then turned her head to seek his mouth again. He gave it to her, his response sending shafts of need lancing through her. She rose on tiptoe, holding him, her upraised arms lifting her breasts, flattening them against his chest.

Keith felt Ali shudder again, felt its vibrations inside himself, answered her with a moan as he cupped his hands around her buttocks and drew her higher against him.

Her scent enflamed him. Her taste engulfed him. Her body, moving in a sexy rhythm, acted as an incendiary to needs too long suppressed. Her hands roved over him, sliding across his chest as he leaned her back against the table, pressing his mouth to the hot, rapid pulse in her neck.

She made a sound and he drew her back upright, still holding her. She slipped free, and slowly, her gaze never leaving his face, began to unbutton her blouse.

"Ali... What are you doing?"

"Seducing you." She shrugged out of her blouse. Her torn skirt was next. She shimmied out of her half-slip, standing before him in nothing but her panties, bra and a blush that rose from tummy to hairline.

He continued to gaze at her, troubled, torn by his own desire for her and his deep need to protect her, if even from herself. He knew she was shy. He knew she was inexperienced, despite having been married. The distance she had traveled already tonight must seem vast to her. Assertiveness training? Did she think, for God's sake, she'd already graduated?

Yet, to his surprise, she unbuttoned his shirt, slid it off his shoulders, then reached up and kissed him again, softly, experimentally, molding her body to his, bare skin to bare skin. A shudder coursed through him.

"Ali..." He kissed her deeply, undid her bra, slid it away, wanting to give her more pleasure than she'd ever known, flooded with a tenderness that made his knees go weak and his head swim. A shudder coursed through her as she swayed against him; a small sound escaped from her. Her fingers locked around his wrists, slid up to his biceps and he stroked his hand down her back, molding her to him.

Her murmurs of delight sent shafts of heat through him. As her lips parted, he accepted the invitation. Her tongue met his, thrust for generous thrust. The fingers of her left hand tangled in his hair, while her right slipped inside the waist of his jeans, spreading over his buttocks.

Ali felt the vibration of his groan inside herself, answered it with a swiftly indrawn breath, then moaned his name as he drew her higher against him. His hands cupped around her buttocks, sliding inside her panties, slipping them down. Heat flared instantly over her skin, scorching her, as did his gusty exhalation.

His scent enflamed her. His taste engulfed her. Her hands roved over him, sliding up his chest, her fingers spreading across his shoulders, flexing, digging into his muscles. His breath came moist and rapid against her neck as he tore his mouth from hers and leaned his head back, gasping for air before lowering it again and nibbling at her lips with small, hot kisses that she returned, one by one, nipping with her teeth, soothing with her tongue, then kissing him back again.

Her trembling knees threatened to buckle, but he

held her tightly, keeping them both upright, when all Ali wanted was to lie on the floor, on the table, anywhere, and draw him into her. Her hands went to his belt buckle, and with a jerk, he moved back.

"No! Sweetheart, no. I don't have anything with me to protect you."

Ali, feeling very brave, smiled. "I," she said, picking up the little drugstore bag he'd taken from her grocery bag, and dangled it in front of him, "I have something to protect you."

While he watched, she opened it, took out the contents and laid the box on his hand. "I hope this brand suits you?"

He caught her close, burying his laughter in her hair, then lifted her and carried her to her bedroom. This time, he made no objection when she unbuckled his belt, slid down his zipper and pushed his jeans down over his hips.

He helped her, then lay beside her. Holding her close, he slowly, sweetly, aroused their passion to a towering pitch.

Then, just before they had reached the point of no return, he rolled to a sitting position. "Are you sure about this?" he whispered.

"Very sure," she replied, and knelt before him, between his knees. She had never been more sure of anything else in her life.

He buried his face against her shoulder.

"I'm not talking just about making love tonight," he said. "I'm talking about our... relationship, Ali. I want...so much." He lifted his head and gazed at her, swallowed visibly. "Maybe too much. Maybe too soon."

"I want a lot, too," she said. He would, naturally, have to go back to his job. She still had every intention of doing her own world explorations. But she wanted this, needed this, him, more than she'd ever needed anything else in her life. "Do you really think denying ourselves—this—would make it any easier?"

He levered her back from him. "Yes. No. Oh, hell, I don't know. All I know is that we should slow down, and that I'm the one who has to do it because I'm the—"

She lay her arms along his thighs, hands on his hips. "You're the what? The man? The man who gets to choose the type of paint we use, the quality of the sail, the manufacturer of the mast, to make all the decisions about what's right, not only for the boat, but for the relationship?

"I conceded all those other things, because I knew you knew more about the boat than I did. But it doesn't work here, Keith. I know more about me than you do."

"But—" He'd been about to say, *But I'm the one with the most to lose,* when he realized she was right. She did know herself better than he did. Even if he was the one with the most to lose, he was probably also the one with the most to gain. "It's not like that," he said.

"Well, then, what is it like?" she asked, but he had no answer.

"You don't know?" she asked. "Then let's find out, Keith. Together." She reached for the box he'd put on the bedside table and opened it deliberately, then sat staring in confusion at the tightly sealed foil envelope she found. "Heavens," she said. "I thought we had laws about overpackaging!"

"Oh...hell!" His soft explosion of laughter got half buried in her breasts. "Ali, Ali..." He tumbled them both backward onto the bed. "You're killing me, woman. You never stop surprising me."

"Good," she said, wrapping her arms around him, feeling his laughter shake through him as joy pulsed through her. "I dread the day when you grow bored with me. I want to keep on surprising you, pleasing you, as long as I can. I—" His kiss stopped her words, stopped her heart, stopped her breath.

"Love me," she whispered. "Make love with me—and don't be afraid of the future. Tonight, it doesn't exist."

He showed her how to open the foil package, then set its contents aside. "Don't we need it?" she asked.

"Not yet," he murmured. "Not until you're really ready."

She thought she already was, but his care and tenderness drove her passions higher and higher. He kissed her until she was dizzy with wanting him. He stroked her body until she thought her skin would burst into flame, until she writhed and begged him to stop, then not to stop, never to stop. He lay back and sat her astride his hips while he continued to caress her.

He'd take care of her, he promised. He'd never, never hurt her. She was so delicate, so dainty; he loved her ears, her spangly gold eyelashes. He kissed them while he slid his hands over the curve of her hips, up past the narrowness of her waist, to the fullness of her breasts. She quivered in pleasure, but he mistook it for a shiver of cold and wrapped his arms around her, enfolding her in his warmth. He rolled until he lay atop her and drew the cover over her back. "I'm not cold," she told him.

He rubbed his hands gently on her arms. "You have goose bumps."

She drew her nails lightly down his sides. "I know. You gave them to me." Then, not so lightly, she raked them over him again, and slid out from under him. She sat up and touched his chest. "Now let me give you some."

"Lie down," he said as goose bumps popped up all over his arms and legs. "Let me love you, Ali."

"You always want to do everything," she said teasingly as she shoved him onto his back. She had a goal and intended to reach it by the shortest possible route.

He chuckled. "Damn right. I mean to do everything. To you, Ali. With you."

She laughed softly, small bursts of warmth and sound against his mouth when she bent to kiss him.

"Ladies first." Now astride him, she tunneled her fingers through the thick hair on his chest and found his nipples. They peaked. "You have the most magnificent shoulders," she murmured, and paid homage to them with her hands and lips. He dragged in an unsteady breath.

"Ali." She watched him swallow. "Do you know what it does to me—inside—when you say things like that?"

"I hope it makes you feel good."

"It—" He closed his eyes. "Yes, dammit, it makes me feel good." She could tell the admission surprised him. Hadn't any of his other women ever paid him compliments? Had they been blind? Completely insensitive to the most basic of human needs after food and shelter; the need to be loved, the need for approval?

"What does that make me," he asked, gazing at her, his dark eyes oddly vulnerable. "Totally conceited, self-centered, egotistical?"

"No." She smiled. "Totally human."

Sliding her hands up beside his neck she massaged his shoulder muscles again. "Does that feel good, too?"

His eyes wide open, he gazed at her, a half smile curving his lips. "Hell, yes!" His hips thrust upward, lifting her as she sat astride him, parting her thighs wider. "Everything about you makes me feel good." He clamped his hands over her thighs, high, his thumbs pressing into the V of her legs, moving gently, rising to meet in the center. She shuddered and pressed against them.

"That..." she said raggedly, "makes me feel good."

Under his touch, she felt her pulse accelerate. She bent forward and brushed her mouth over his, stroking her tongue across his lips. They opened, firmed, and he fisted a hand in the back of her hair, holding her still while he took command of the kiss. She let him control it for a moment only, then broke free, taking his hand and placing it at his side again. There was so much she needed to do, so much she wanted to give. And there was plenty of time. Tonight, she had no intention of complying with her self-imposed ten-thirty bedtime, at least not for sleep.

"I can make you feel even better," Keith said, cupping her breasts in his hands, squeezing gently. "Let me make you feel better than you've ever felt in your life, Ali, the way you make me feel."

"You do," she whispered, bending to nuzzle the skin under his ear, fitting herself more securely into his palms. "Oh, you do, but ladies first, remember?"

His voice grated in her ear. "Maybe ladies get to go first, but you're one lady who better make it fast, or it's going to be game over in about ten seconds." He tweaked her nipples.

With a moan of pleasure, she lifted up and spread her palms over his chest, smiling when his nipples popped to attention under her hands. Bending, she kissed one, then the other, hearing his breath hiss in past his teeth. She scraped a nail down the center of his chest to his navel and felt a fresh crop of goose bumps pop up on his skin. She rubbed one set away with her hand, the other with her cheek. "Cold?" she murmured.

"Burning..."

"Good." She bit his shoulder gently, nibbled at his neck, then lightly encircled his erection with her hand.

"Don't!" he gasped, as he wrapped her arm tightly in his hand and flipped her over, lying half on top of her. Ali stared up at him, her hands in his hair, her lips parted, her breath coming fast. "Why not? What do you want me to do?"

"Everything!" he promised. "Everything, but I want my turn, too."

The heat of Keith's mouth engulfed Ali's breasts, bringing her body into a tight arch as she rose to fill his need, let him fill hers. His stomach muscles rippled at her touch and he made a ragged sound that affected her as deeply as the most intimate touch. She felt the hot rigidity of his erection under her fingers as she slowly unrolled protection over him. He went very still until she finished, his arms shaking as he held himself above her, watching her hands on his body.

"Did I do it right?" she asked.

He didn't answer, but as he came to her, the hair of his thighs deliciously rough against her legs, she knew she must have. She slid one leg up over him, holding him with it, holding him with her arms, her hands around his head now, his mouth on her body, moving from breast to breast. He caressed her abdomen, sending spasms of pleasure through her, turning her soft and liquid inside.

He dipped into the well of her center, and her hips lifted in an involuntary surge seeking deeper contact.

"You feel so good to me," he murmured, before taking her mouth again. His tongue mimicked the action of his fingers and Ali's mind spun out of control. She tore her mouth free, buried her face against him and sobbed for him to stop, to let her breathe, but he continued, keeping her hovering on the edge of ecstasy.

"I want you," she whispered. "I need you, Keith..."

"Yes!" He gasped the word then, with a hoarse cry he lifted her knees, and drove deep into her.

"Yes!" Her cry mingled with his groan. Her legs wrapped around him. Her fingers dug into the taut muscles of his buttocks as he lifted her higher, plunging deeper, again, again, again, and then one last time while they both trembled and cried out.

"Ah, Ali, sweetheart," he said in what seemed a long time later. He had rolled so that he lay on the mattress, and she lay on top of him. He ran his hands over her back.

"Baby, I'm sorry. I'm so sorry."

She had to bring herself back from a different plane of existence. "Sorry?"

"I lost my head. I forgot everything but my own needs."

Ali laughed, dropping her face down into the angle between his shoulder and neck, breathing in the warm scent of his skin. She slipped off him, and lay by his side with her head on his shoulder. "Isn't it wonderful," she said, smoothing her hand over his chest, "that your needs and mine are exactly the same?"

"Not exactly," he said. He sighed softly, tucked his arm over her and rolled toward her, nestling her close. As she drifted into sleep, she thought she heard him whisper that he loved her, but maybe it was just the beginnings of a dream. She wanted to ask him if he'd said it, if he'd meant it, but the dream took over completely and she slid into its welcome depths, not to waken until a heavy hammering on her door disturbed an unusually erotic dream.

9

ALI STAGGERED OUT, tying her robe as she went. Blinking sleep from her eyes, staring up at Keith. "What's wrong?" A glance at the wall over the kitchen stove told her it was only ten past six.

Keith ran a hand over her tousled hair, tucking a wisp of it behind her ear. "The only thing wrong I can see is you're not exactly dressed to launch a boat."

"I'm not due to get up for another half hour!"

He grinned unsympathetically as he slid his hands inside her robe. "I know this is outside your routine, Ali, but wasn't last night, too?"

A long, shaky breath escaped her. Last night had been anything but routine! "I haven't even been to sleep," he said, "and the boat is all ready to go."

"Not sleep? Why?"

"Because there was more pleasure in watching you sleep until dawn. Then, I did some heavy thinking. After that, I called my magazine's editorial offices in Geneva, Switzerland." He went silent for a moment, gazing at her intently, then added softly, "I'm no longer on vacation, Ali. I quit."

"Quit?"

"Right. So we're both unemployed. Come on," he urged. "Let's go sailing. I have two thermoses of coffee onboard, plus a breakfast even you'd approve of, and the breeze is up. What are you waiting for, woman? Let's roll!"

She drew a deep breath and said, "Give me half an hour."

His hands, still inside her robe, made some interesting maneuvers. She released a shuddering sigh. He pulled the belt undone, bent and put his mouth over one of her breasts. After a moment, he lifted his head, his gaze burning into hers. "I think you're going to need a little more than half an hour. And it's not right, forcing a woman to break routine."

He turned her and directed her back to her bedroom. "Go back to bed, Ali."

She looked at him over her shoulder, through a tangle of messy hair. "Are you going to join me?"

He was close on her heels. "In more ways than one."

LAST NIGHT'S LOVING had been long, languorous and exploratory. This morning's was totally different, an instant burning need meeting instant burning need, a swift and potent joining of bodies and passions and a fierce, almost frantic blending of emotions. It left Ali in tears of joy, and Keith limp, as he put it, all over.

"I don't know," he said, "if I'll be able to hoist a sail for about twelve hours."

Ali giggled. "Probably not. The mast seems to have collapsed."

He was still laughing against her throat, while the "mast" made valiant attempts at reasserting itself, when the phone began to ring.

It was precisely six forty-five.

Everyone knew that Ali would by now have had her shower and be well into her first cup of coffee.

The first call was from her mother, who had just read the morning paper. She wanted to assure herself Ali was unhurt, she wanted to know all about Keith, how serious the relationship was, and could she start buying more items for Ali's trousseau anytime soon. "That looked like quite a kiss."

Kiss? In the *paper?* Ali dropped the phone to the bedside table, and quite oblivious of her naked state, dashed out and grabbed the paper off the porch. Back in her bedroom, she scanned it while her mother continued to comment and question, and Keith made far too many efforts to distract her.

The front page carried a picture of a reporter picking himself up off the ground while Keith and Ali, hand in hand, ran for his vehicle.

Renowned Photographer Saves Librarian, one headline read. The article was partly factual, but mostly wrong, and quoted Ali as stating "hysterically" that she'd enjoyed the experience so much she was looking for more adventure. A small photograph of Keith kissing her suggested that was the kind of additional adventure she was seeking.

Ali denied. She argued, she promised her mother she had no intention of needing a trousseau anytime soon and that Keith's kiss had been purely to shut her up because he thought she was saying weird things.

Which, her mother agreed, she certainly had. "Travel? Ali, you won't even go to Vancouver shopping with me unless I coerce you. What makes you think you can go to Ecuador or Greece?"

"Greece?" Ali echoed. "Where did that come in? It's not in the paper."

"Ruth Rathbury claims you and her great-nephew are planning a trip there. Believe me, she doesn't approve. She called me about it at least two weeks ago. I've been waiting for you to own up."

"There's nothing to own up to! I'm taking a trip to Ecuador and I'm going alone, Mom. Keith Devon is a photojournalist who goes around taking pictures and writing stories of horrible war scenes. And now, I don't want to talk about it anymore. Please!"

With that, she hung up, and gave in to the sensations Keith had been inducing with small kisses, expert caresses and seductive whispers. "Hey, remember?" he said. "I'm no longer a photojournalist who takes distressing pictures and writes true-horror stories. I'm unemployed, but I think I've found my new career—making Ali wriggle."

Dammit, who was supposed to be seducing whom, here?

But she could no more have stopped what was happening than she could have stopped breathing. Finally, as more and more calls from incredulous people, laughing people, scoffing people continued to pour in, none of them willing to believe she would so much as travel to Kamloops, let alone Ecuador, she shut off the phone and let her answering machine take care of it until it literally danced with frenetic red lights.

"Let's go sailing," she said, and Keith agreed at once, though for the past half hour, listening to her assure everyone she had meant exactly what she said, that she was definitely going to be taking some tours, he'd become more and more quiet.

Halfway around the lake, he pulled the boat into a secluded little cove, anchored and suggested a swim. Ali glanced down at her shorts and T-shirt, and bit her lip. "I'm not exactly dressed for swimming."

He grinned and stripped off his shirt, then his shorts, stood on the side of the boat and dived over. Surfacing, he grinned up at her. "The trick," he said, "is to get *un*dressed for swimming."

Ali's stare widened as she thought about it. Keith saw that delightful blush he'd come to love rise up over her face, intensifying the blue of her eyes, while the sun made golden spangles on her lashes, and created a halo around her head.

"There's no one around, love," he said. "Just you and me." He thought of the joy he'd know if he could have this, just this, for the rest of his life. *Just you and me...*

He watched her swallow, watched her stand, watched her pull her T-shirt off, then her shorts. He hardened, but kept silent while she hesitated over her bra and panties, but then, in two quick motions, she rid herself of both those garments and flung herself into the water with him.

He caught her to him, feeling the lake-cooled globes of her breasts press against his chest. Her arms went around his neck, her legs floated up around his waist and he held her, reveling in the nearness of her body, the trust she had placed in him. Maybe now was the time to tell her.

He would have, but she kissed him then, and all he could do was grab on to the anchor chain to keep them afloat while their wet, sleek bodies did what wet, sleek bodies did best, joined and rejoined until they were both deliciously spent.

Once back aboard the boat, they rubbed each other dry with towels, dressed again between kisses and caresses, then pulled the anchor, set the sail and headed back toward Mitikiltuk.

"There is something I want to show you," Keith said. "Something I want to discuss with you. We can do it over lunch on the terrace of the Old Hotel."

"I'VE BOUGHT THE HOTEL," Keith said, after their wine had been poured, and while they waited for their meal to arrive.

Ali stared at him. His face was shaded by the umbrella under which they sat, but for all that, she was certain there was nothing but seriousness in his eyes.

"Well, maybe I haven't bought it, not yet, not exactly, but I've made an offer that's been accepted, and all that I have to wait for is the paperwork to be completed. Signing should be in less than a month."

Ali could say nothing. She took a gulp of her wine and nearly choked. "Why?" she whispered.

"Because I like it. I like the location. I see a lot of potential. Did you know that, even in the high season, they're running at less than fifty percent occupancy rate? And in the winter, it's even less."

"You want to buy a losing proposition?"

"I want to turn it into a paying proposition."

Ali looked around at the blue hair, the bald heads, the slow, ponderous games of chess, the tables of bridge players, the few desultorily shoving shuffleboard disks down a long table inside the main activity room. Where would they all go for their summer vacations if the Old Mitikiltuk Hotel became the New Mitikiltuk Hotel? Would Keith put in a karaoke machine? Would he have Western Nights, and Happy Hours, and Mystery Weekends to attract younger, more lively guests?

"How?" she said. "How do you plan to turn it into a paying proposition?"

"With your help, Ali. I've given this a lot of thought. There are several poorly designed spaces, nooks and crannies that have no apparent use—they're too big to be turned into guest rooms, yet too small to become conference rooms. I see them as reading areas, filled with books and comfortable chairs and good lighting. There are three floors, with two such spaces on each floor, plus another larger one on the ground floor between the billiards room and the main lounge."

"Books for the guests to read, or to buy?"

"To read while they're here. Most of them book for the full summer season, but the reading rooms would also be open to the public, with regular lending privileges. Mitikiltuk needs a library. Aunt Ruth says she, for one, won't be able to drive to K'ville in the winter when the roads are snowy or icy, and there are many others who feel the same. Maybe we could tie in with the K'ville library and do what they call interlibrary loans if people request material we don't have."

"You want to turn the hotel into a library?"

"No. I want to keep it as a hotel. But I want to make use of the space that's being wasted, want to make it even more attractive than it is. As for the low occupancy rate in the winter, we could attract cross-country skiers, maybe even hook in with a heliskiing operation, get people here during that season, too. Mitikiltuk Lake freezes over. We could host skating competitions, community hockey games. There are dozens of possibilities."

"What...what do you know about being a hotelier?"

He laughed and sat back as the waitress set a shrimp salad in front of each of them, then topped off their glasses from the bottle in the wine bucket.

"Not a hell of a lot," he admitted. "But there are people who do, people we could hire to manage that end of it. The present owner's no chef, either, but he's always managed to keep his guests fed."

Ali laughed. "Not always well." She glanced down at the table, then back up at him. "The night you bullied me into dining here with you, I was hoping they'd have their usual gruesome fare and you'd never ask me out again, but wouldn't you know it, the food was great."

"And so were you. So are you. And I didn't bully you."

"Did, too!"

"Did not! I merely...persuaded you."

"By threatening me with my picture in the paper." She laughed again. "Which I ended up with anyway, despite myself."

His eyes sobered. His voice dropped. "You've done a lot of things, Ali, despite yourself, and I believe you can do this, too, with me. We can do it, Ali. We can make it work. It'll use up most of my savings, buying the place and putting it in order, but nobody ever said you have to rich to be happy."

She nibbled a piece of shrimp. "You keep saying 'we.'"

He leaned forward, intense. "Yes, Ali. We. You and I. Look, I know you want to travel, have some adventures, some challenges. I know this might not be the kind of challenge you thought you wanted, so I'm not asking for a commitment right this minute. You need time to think about it."

Did she? A large part of Ali wanted to say she didn't, but then she couldn't help wondering if that was the old, cowardly Ali showing up again, taking the easy way out, going for something that would ...much closer to her normal routine. What, she wondered, would Katerina think if she wimped out now and let herself be led around by the nose?

But was she in danger of being led around by the nose, or in even worse danger of being lead by her heart? She'd done that once before, and look where it had gotten her. It had gotten her miserable and unhappy and even less sure of herself and her abilities than before.

Keith was right. She did have to think.

"I may not know much about hotel-keeping," he said, "but I do know about people. I saw you looking around at the old dears who inhabit this place. You were thinking I might mean to turn it into a place they can't afford, or won't be comfortable in."

She nodded.

"I don't plan to do that. I won't do it, with you beside me to keep me on track. You know its history, you know its value to the community and you know books. Your running the reading rooms, the library end of it is all that will make it possible for it to go."

"Keith—"

"No," he said, wrapping his hand around hers. "Drink your wine, eat your salad and we'll talk about other things. This can wait. As I said, the papers aren't even signed."

He grinned as he picked up her fork and held out a shrimp for her to eat. "Besides, we have a newly refurbished catboat floating down there at the dock, and a whole lot more lake to explore."

Then he slyly added, "And maybe some more swimming to do?"

She blushed as he fed her a shrimp, then took control of her own fork.

She wished it was as easy to take control of her own life.

THE SAILING, the swimming, the loving, were wonderful over the next few days. Now and then, one or the other of them would mention the hotel, bring up a suggestion, toss it around for a while, then tuck it away for future reference.

Ali found herself making lists, lists of must-have books, lists of departments, lists of which should go where. The children's corner, of course, would need to be on the main floor, in a bright, cheerful location, with lots of low tables and cushions and carpets and teddy bears for children to hug while being read stories to.

Then she'd tuck the lists away because none of it was really real anyway, at least not yet, and maybe never would be. Most of the time she was busy learning about other things, anyway.

She discovered the delights of being the captain, of giving the orders to her crew, of handling the boat by herself. She found that sailing by moonlight was total magic as was the silence of the world while everyone but she and Keith slept.

She learned to love swimming at night, too, and wondered why she had never done it; why she had never swum *naked* before.

She deeply luxuriated in the sensuality of the

water against her skin. She laughed aloud. She wished she were a dolphin, wished she could stay this way forever.

The slide of the warm, silky water past her naked body was enlivening, exciting. She ducked down and swam underwater, feeling it caress her hair, sliding through like gentle fingers. She surfaced, rolled onto her back and floated near the dock, hands and feet fluttering only enough to keep her from sinking.

High overhead, the stars wheeled slowly. The moon that had earlier risen over the hills to the east was about to disappear behind the trees in the west. A faint sound caused her to turn her head.

Keith swam not two feet from her.

He swept a hand slowly toward her, touched her fingertips with his and it was like no other touch she had ever experienced. Knowing they were both naked, clothed only in water and shadows, added an erotic twist to their contact.

She went still in the water, allowing her feet to sink until her toes just touched the sand. Turning, she faced Keith, maintaining that light connection of fingertip to fingertip. With infinite care, as if to be too bold would break the spell, she linked her fingers with his and drew his hand to her bare breast.

His fingers trembled. The warmth of his skin against her cool flesh popped her nipple into a hard, aching bead.

"Ali..." His voice was a faint whisper.

"What?" Hers was little more.

"You're playing with fire," he warned her.

"Doesn't water quench fire?"

He came closer, slid his other hand around the back of her neck. "Not in this case." He drew her to him, her toes left the sand and she floated into his arms, supported only by his caressing hand on her breast, his other on her nape.

"Oh!" She gasped and trembled violently as their bodies achieved full, frontal contact. It was all she could do to prevent her legs parting and floating up around him.

"Do you want the fire quenched?" he asked, easing back from her, letting her go until her feet found bottom again.

"How would you intend to go about doing that?"

"Ali..." Keith couldn't go on, could only look at her, scarcely able to breathe. Her hair lay flat and close to her head. The waning moonlight spread a sheen over it. She lifted an arm to brush a dripping lock back from her face, tucking it behind her ear. The action lifted one perfect, round breast, one delightfully pointed nipple, one graceful arm, free of the water.

She was Eve, Circe, Lorelei, Delilah, every temptress ever created rolled into one. And he loved her.

He wanted to cup his hands around her face, and tell her. He wanted to stroke his thumbs over the curves of her cheeks, close those eyes of hers that somehow burned into his soul—even here in the dark. Never before had he been so captivated by a woman's eyes. He wanted to draw her back to him so their naked forms melded together, wanted to part her lips, plunge into her, open her mouth for his own pleasure, and for hers. But more, he wanted to slide his hands down her body, over her hips, her thighs, lift them, part them, wrap them around him and accept her offer of loving.

But was it that for her? She had never said anything to indicate it was more for her than recreational sex. Even when they talked about the hotel, she kept the conversations impersonal, as if potential business partner to potential business partner, or potential employee to hotel owner.

And in all the times they'd been together like this, loving, the word "love" had never passed between them. He wanted to say it. He wanted to very badly, but he'd never said it before to any other woman, and it was such a difficult phrase to force out. Especially in the face of Ali's ebullience yesterday when they'd come home and she'd found her mail lying on the floor in the hallway.

She'd danced around, her crazy, wind-tossed hair that he'd unpinned the minute they got aboard the boat, flying around her head and shoulders. She'd hugged something to her chest, an expression of ecstasy on her face.

"My passport," she'd whispered in awe. With trembling hands, she'd opened it, looked at the photo, seemed pleased even with that, then stared at her Ecuador visa stamp. Tears had filled her eyes, spilled over and she'd flung herself into his arms, laughing and crying with delight.

How could he now tell her how much he loved her, how desperately he wanted her not to go away?

For a moment, he felt a surge of outrage. How could she appeal to him so strongly on all the different levels she did, and be prepared to reject whatever he might offer her beyond the "vacation fling" she had claimed not to want, but which might now be all she wanted from him?

But whatever she wanted from him, he wanted whatever she might offer. Together, they waded from the water, wrapped themselves in their robes and went to her house, where her bed and the candles she would light, awaited them.

Keith swore that for the moment, it would be enough.

HE AWOKE long before full daybreak, and lay listening to Ali breathe beside him. As dawn lightened the sky, he could make out her features. He traced them carefully with an index finger, loving the shape of her nose, her cheeks, her pointed chin. She woke, slowly, stretching, rubbing herself against him as if she were a cat, and they made slow, languid love at daybreak. Then, with a smile, she fell asleep again.

Keith rose, went to the bathroom and wandered into the kitchen to put on coffee for her before leaving to go back to his aunt's house. He was always careful to give the impression of having spent the night in his own bed. Aunt Ruth was of a different generation, and despite her desire to see him and Ali as a couple, he still felt the need to protect Ali's reputation in her small hometown.

He smiled. Her small hometown that was about to become his small hometown.

As he walked past the kitchen table, a terrible odor made him wrinkle his nose. What could that be?

He checked the fridge, the counter, the cupboards, nothing. The smell seemed centered at the area of the table. He looked under it. Looked under the cloth, grinning in remembrance of that first morning and the tablecloth he'd put on to make himself decent for Ali. How far they'd come since then!

In one side of the table, he found the source of the smell. Pulling out the small drawer there, he found a notebook, stained with something, covered in mold, and reeking badly. About to throw it into the garbage can outside, he flipped it open to see if it contained anything important, since Ali was always making lists.

His own name caught his eye, along with a big, bold check mark at the bottom of a list entitled Things To Do To Achieve Personal Growth.

There it was, number five: *Seduce Keith Devon so I'll have a great memory to take on my travels, and some experience to use should the occasion ever arise again.*

He heard again her semihysterical voice after that terrible abduction, saying she was Ali the Hun, saying she could do anything now, face the world, seduce him.

Seduce him! As part of her personal development plan. As part of her assertiveness training course. So that's all he was here—

Angry and sick at heart, he flung the smelly notebook back onto the table, still open to the damning page. He got her passport from where she'd stood it in a place of pride on the mantel, as if it were a Christmas card from a lover, and slapped it down beside the notebook.

He picked up a pen and wrote, "Have a good trip," signed it "Number Five," and then marched out.

Before the sun had fully risen, he was packed up and gone, thanking his lucky stars he hadn't actually signed any final papers on the deal for the hotel. Or said any irrecoverable words to Ali Kozinski.

ALI WOKE to the sound of a vehicle burning rubber outside her house. Curious, she got up and went downstairs.

In the kitchen, she found her notebook, her passport and Keith's curt, cruel little note.

He hadn't so much as given her a chance to explain.

She rushed to the street side of the house, but his Bronco was gone. She could see the black streaks his tires had left as he peeled out.

To go where?

Back to his exciting, scary, but obviously preferred war zones? She should have known she could never hold a man like Keith Devon, nor could a town like Mitikiltuk. He was too impetuous, too passionate, too...angry. And he'd never given her a chance to explain!

THAT THOUGHT kept her going while she readied her house for her absence. By ten o'clock, her fridge was cleaned out, her newspaper stopped, her light timers set to come on and turn off in random patterns, and her suitcase lay open on her bed. By eleven, Ali was packed and in her car, heading south to Vancouver. She'd call her mother from there.

She had no idea what time she could get a flight out, or even which airline to approach. But it didn't matter. She was on her way and whatever happened from this point on, would happen because she, Ali the Hun, had made it happen. For herself. Because she, if no one else in the world did, believed in herself.

10

"SORRY, MISS, it's just not that easy." It was perhaps the fifth time Ali had heard that phrase or one similar in the past half hour.

"What, then, would make it easy?" she said in her best and calmest Katerina Boyd manner.

"Well, you could take a flight to San Francisco. That would get you in there at 11:40 tonight. You'd have a six-hour layover before boarding a flight for Mexico City. From there, you might get a flight to Quito within the next three or four days, or possibly within the hour. It all depends."

"Depends on what?"

"Variables. How over-or underbooked they are. And—" the man leaned closer across the counter "—it often depends on how much of a, shall we say, 'tip' you're prepared to offer."

"Bribe, you mean."

"Miss, things are done differently in Latin America. Now, shall I book you on this flight for San Francisco or not?"

Ali took it. Her layover there was closer to nine hours than six, but she didn't dare leave the airport to find a bed somewhere, regardless of how exhausted she was. When she arrived in Mexico City, she prayed for a layover of at least twenty-four hours, because she was reeling from lack of sleep. However, she learned that if she were to board a flight leaving within the next hour for Bogotá, Colombia, she could be in Quito by the next afternoon.

"I'll sleep on the plane," she muttered, after the ticket agent assured her her luggage would be automatically transferred. "Just try to get me a window seat."

With a thin pillow between her and the small window, and a blanket draped over her, she slipped into an uneasy doze after they had reached cruising altitude. Into her sleep crept the memory of Keith's hand sliding up her thigh. She moved slightly—toward him. A scent quite unlike Keith wafted over her, and a voice whispered something unintelligible into her ear.

She awoke with a jolt, smashed the exploring hand off her leg, and shoved her garlic-loving seatmate back into his own space. He blinked, and pretended to have fallen asleep himself, apologizing profusely for his "mistake."

Ali didn't dare close her eyes the rest of the way to Bogotá, where luckily, she got to change planes and leave the garlic lover behind.

The next leg went slightly more smoothly, except for the acrid smell of tobacco smoke that permeated the cabin, along with the scent of rancid fat from some kind of stew the fat lady next to her spooned out of a plastic margarine container, offering Ali a bite every couple of minutes, despite her repeated refusals.

Landing in Quito was like landing in a steam-bath. Ali realized within moments of stepping off the air-conditioned plane, that she'd never truly had a bad-hair day in her life. Here, despite the "comfortable" climate the altitude of this city was supposed to provide, her hair went into immediate rebellion, popping the few pins that were left, and spreading itself around her head as if it were an electrically charged porcupine.

She waited, and waited, and waited in vain for her suitcase to appear. Crates with chickens in them came down the chute. One with a goat in it, another with a motorcycle. Bags of all descriptions were snatched up and toted away by people who talked too loud and too fast and completely unintelligibly. What was even worse, was a pair of guards armed with rifles who seemed to be taking much too great an interest in her as she waited. When the carousel had gone around three times empty but for one little gray case, which an elderly nun finally picked up, Ali realized her luggage was not going to appear.

Try though she did, she could not make her needs understood. She got voluble babbles, many shrugs and hand tosses for her efforts, but no suitcase. Even the airline representative, who claimed to speak English, did so with such an accent Ali could understand maybe one word in ten. None of which helped.

Finally, in desperation, she wandered outside

into the oppressive heat, stood on a curb near a taxi stand and waited for one to appear. Of course, all the other passengers had taken the ones that had met the plane, and she had nearly melted into a puddle of despair when one came meandering slowly along the frontage road.

Quickly she stepped out and waved her arm in what she hoped would be recognized as an assertive manner. As the taxi swerved toward her, a boy on a bicycle swept in beside it, reached out one hand and slashed the strap of her shoulder bag. He had snatched it and was thirty feet away before she could so much as suck in a gulp of the overheated air.

For the second time in her life, Ali let out a shriek of pure rage. She literally vaulted over the hood of the taxi and flew off in pursuit of the bicycle bandit. Whether it was adrenaline or desperation, she didn't know, but catching that boy became the most important thing in her life.

Her feet flew. Her heart pounded, her hair flopped into her eyes but she pushed it out, shouting, screaming and cussing as she ran. He glanced over his shoulder and that might have been his undoing, because by the time he reached the cross street, a slow-moving bus came lumbering in front of him. Ali flung herself at his back wheel just as he tried to pedal around the rear of the bus. She knocked him down, snatched her purse back, smacked him over the head with it and continued to yell until the taxi driver pulled her away and another man in some kind of uniform dragged the boy to his feet.

"Come, missy. Come, missy," the taxi driver said, leading Ali back to his cab, which was blocking an entire stream of impatiently honking cars, trucks and buses.

It reminded her immediately of the day Keith had stopped her at Mitikiltuk's single traffic light. She ached with longing for his special kind of "bullying." She ached with longing for him. If he had been there, that creep on the plane wouldn't have touched her that way. If he had been there, he'd have sensed menace from the boy on the bicycle. If he had been there…

She wiped tears and sweat off her face with the back of one hand.

"I take you fine hotel, missy," the driver assured her, his mustache twitching as he leered at her in the mirror. "Nice hotel for lady. My own brother run hotel. Highly recommended."

Even without Keith, Ali could sense the menace in that.

"No," she said, and dug into her bag. "This hotel." She shoved a slip of paper over the seat back to him. "This hotel and no other."

He glanced at the paper, shrugged dramatically and turned the taxi around.

The name of the hotel he took her to matched the name on the paper, and seemed to be a fairly decent place. She paid him with the small amount of cash she had in her purse, her traveler's checks being stowed "safely" in her now-missing luggage.

Ali brought out an internationally recognized credit card, which the clerk examined as if it must be counterfeit, then handed back. "Please, lady?"

"I have a reservation." She gave her name, which didn't appear to mean a thing to the clerk. She showed him her airline ticket, her booking reservation, and asked to be shown to her room. He spread his hands helplessly.

"Look," she said, striving for patience. "I've had a long, involved and terrible trip getting here. The airline lost my luggage and I need to buy a change of clothing at the very least. I need a bath and some decent food and a bed in that order. Now, please, have someone show me to my room."

The desk clerk looked at her as if she were speaking Martian. "Please, lady?"

"My room. I want my room."

"Please, lady?"

Oh, Lord! Was this what she'd been warned about? Wasn't he going to give her a room until she bribed him? But she couldn't. She'd used all but a few cents paying the taxi driver. Until she got hold of her luggage and her traveler's checks, and her phrase book, which was also in her suitcase, she was stuck. What was she going to do? Camp out in the lobby?

What would Katerina do? She'd stand there and continue to insist, politely and firmly. What would Keith do? She nearly sobbed aloud. Keith would jump over that marble-topped counter and throttle the desk clerk until he could no longer even croak the phrase, "Please, lady."

Why had she ever written that stupid list? Why hadn't she destroyed it? Why had she left it lying around for him to find and come to the wrong conclusion about her? Well, the right one, she supposed, wanting to be honest with herself, but that was before she'd known she'd fallen helplessly, irrevocably in love with him.

She'd almost begun to believe he felt the same, when suddenly, he was gone, and now she was here. Without him. And she needed him.

But all she had was herself.

She planted both hands on the counter as if she might leap over, put her face right into the clerk's and said, "I have had a very bad day and my patience is at an end. I want someone to call the airline and track down my luggage. I want that returned to me within the next twelve hours or I want everything in my suitcase replaced. And I want the room I have already booked and paid for with this credit card. If you can't handle all that, you get me someone who can. Understand?

"You get me someone who speaks English, Mac, and you do it right this minute! I am a very important person who has come a long way to visit your poor little hotel and I demand the service I've paid for. English! You understand me? English!"

He backed off, saying, "Please, lady. Please lady!"

Ali walked to the middle of the polished lobby floor, bent her knees and sat down. She folded her arms across her chest, kept her gaze pinned on the desk clerk and completely ignored all thc other hotel guests who stopped, looked at her, made comments or asked questions she couldn't understand.

At last, the clerk seemed to understand she had no intention of leaving her two square feet of floor unless he did something. He spoke a couple of words and another man appeared, so quickly Ali knew he must have been right at hand the whole time.

The other man came out from behind the desk, crossed the lobby and looked down at her. "Please, lady?" he said. "I am the manager, at your service. I understand your luggage is lost? How may I help you?"

Ali leaped to her feet and almost fell on his neck in gratitude.

That gratitude didn't last long, though. "Not only is my luggage lost, your clerk seems to have lost my reservation."

He frowned and spread his hands in a helpless shrug while he smiled an apologetic, white-toothed smile. "We have no rooms left."

Of course you don't, she wanted to say. *You gave mine to someone who could pay a bigger bribe.* "I have a reservation."

He shrugged and his mustache twitched. "I can only apologize. I have no more rooms. Perhaps it was at another hotel?"

"My reservation is at this hotel." Ali sat on the floor again, holding her shoulder bag on her lap.

The man stared at her. She stared back at him. Neither moved.

Then, Ali put her bag on the floor, lay down and rested her head on it. "I will sleep here," she said, and closed her eyes.

The silence went on so long she thought he had left. The marble tiles were cold and hard under her hip and shoulder. Her back hurt. Her head ached. She wanted Keith's comforting arms around her. She wanted to be home. She wanted never to have wanted adventure.

"There is one possibility," the manager said.

Ali opened her eyes.

"It is not the room you booked."

Ah! So he was now willing to concede she did have a valid reservation. She sat up.

"You will have to share an adjoining bathroom with another guest."

"It doesn't matter. Just take me to it."

"Yes, lady. Yes, lady. This way, please." He tried to take her shoulder bag and carry it for her, but she refused to relinquish it.

Despite the outward grandeur of the hotel, the elevator was old and creaked and moved at a crawl. Ali leaned against a wall, hoping her legs would hold out until she was able to lie down.

The corridor was long, the carpet thick and dark red. Dim lights seemed lost in the dark wood paneling, but when the man opened a door, sunlight flooded in between slatted shutters.

The air was blessedly cool. Through a closed door, she could hear water splashing into a tub. Her neighbor, it seemed, had beaten her to it. It made her yearn to be in it, but she could wait.

The bed was large and looked antique, and made her yearn just as strongly as the thought of the tub.

"I will have housekeeping bring you a robe and toiletries," he said, and bowed. "Please lady. Be comfortable in our poor little hotel."

She felt almost ashamed of her tantrum now, of having so denigrated his hotel to the clerk. The travel agent she'd seen in San Francisco who had recommended this place had said it was old and well-established, a five-star hotel she'd never regret visiting. Seeing this room told her the woman had been right.

"If I don't answer the door, the maid may leave the robe on the bed," she said. "I will be in the bath as soon as it's free."

"The bath," said a familiar voice behind her, "is free now."

Ali whirled.

"I'll take over from here, Manuel," Keith said. "Thank you for all you have done."

"*Sí,* Señor Devon," the manager said. "Thank you. Thank you, lady." He bowed his way out of the room, closing the door with a gentle click.

"Keith—what—why—how—?"

"Can it wait?" he asked, leading her to the bed and sitting her down.

"For what?"

Ali slipped her sandals off her feet, rubbed her soles, her toes, her insteps. "For this." He stood her on her feet and stripped off her limp blouse, her damp bra. He slid her slacks off over her hips, complete with her panties.

When she was naked, he lifted her and carried her into the bathroom where he lowered her into an enormous tub filled with tepid water. He eased her down, leaned her back against its sloping end, picked up a cake of sweet-scented soap and began to lather her arms, her hands, her legs.

Ali closed her eyes, but even that couldn't stop the tears squeezing out. He bent and brushed them away with his lips, then sat her up and soaped her back.

Presently he lifted her out, wrapped her in a large towel and carried her, not to her room, but to his. He laid her down, pulled the damp towel away and drew a thin, smooth sheet over her. "Sleep," he whispered. "I'll be here when you wake."

Ali didn't doubt it for a minute. When a nightmare turned into a dream, only good things could happen. The best part of this dream was when she awoke to find Keith curled around her as if he were a protective shell for her back, one arm under her waist, one hand cupping a breast.

The clock on the bedside table told her it was nine-thirty in the morning. She must have been exhausted, to sleep so late, she thought, then realized that in her own time zone, it was half-past six in the morning.

She grinned. Right on schedule. Smack along the lines of her normal routine. Except for one major item: Keith, who slept on, even as she gently slid away from him, and out of bed. How had he gotten there? Why was he there? And why did she have the distinct impression he was no longer in a flaming rage about being number five on her list?

In the other room, she was delighted to find her missing luggage, along with a luxurious terry-cloth robe, which she pulled on at once. She brushed her teeth, washed her face, and brushed her hair before twisting it up into its customary knot. Then, with phrase book in hand, she braved the telephone and ordered coffee for immediate delivery and breakfast for two in an hour.

Then, and only then, did she let herself think.

Why was Keith here? She grew light-headed for a minute. Was there about to be some kind of political coup? But no. It wasn't that. Common sense told her Keith was here because she was here. Keith was in the other half of this suite because he had arranged it that way. She didn't know how, she didn't know why, but he was the one responsible for this being the only room available to her in this entire, big hotel where she had booked a single room just for herself. She wondered if, somehow, he'd also arranged for her luggage to go missing.

The question was, why?

Before she could give it much thought, room service arrived and she curled up in a chair by the window with a steaming cup of coffee.

She was halfway through her second cup when Keith came out, wearing a robe similar to hers.

He stood looking at her for a long, silent moment, then poured himself some coffee. He crossed to where she sat and eased himself down onto an ottoman near her chair. Something in his expression filled her with a kind of fear she had never experienced.

She recognized it, though. Dread. He had followed her to make her explain. And she didn't think she could. Not adequately. Never adequately. Never believably.

"I have to say something I've never said before," he told her. "Something I never expected to say."

She set her cup down. "What?"

"I love you," he said.

She gaped at him. "You do?"

"I do. And I want to marry you, spend the rest of my life with you."

He leaned over and slid a hand up her arm under the wide sleeve of her robe. "And I'm sorry for leaving you without giving you a chance to explain that list. It was all part of your course, wasn't it? And it was the scariest thing you could think of in the world."

"It still is," she whispered. "It became even scarier when I realized how much I loved you, and didn't know if you felt the same."

He took a sip from his cup and set it on the carpet. "And now that you do know?"

She wanted to weep. "I'm still afraid you'll get tired of me."

He stood and came to her. "Why would I get tired of you?"

"Because you don't really want a quiet, peaceful woman."

"What's your point?"

"I'm that."

He threw back his head and laughed.

"Ali, you throw dishes. You take on crooks. You won't let hotel desk clerks walk all over you. You demand your rights and get them. I nearly cracked up when I saw you staging that sit-in in the middle of the lobby and above all that, you make love like a houri."

She snatched herself away. "A *what?*"

He laughed again, catching her and holding her. A *houri,*" he said, emphasizing the last syllable, then the rest of what he'd said penetrated.

"You saw me sitting on the floor of the lobby? You knew I was here? You didn't try to help me?"

"No. You were doing fine on your own. I just came back up here and started running your bath because I knew you'd want one."

"You made them withold my room!"

"Guilty as charged. It happens all the time, Ali, to travelers. They have to fight to get what they've paid for. They have to assert themselves just the way you did."

He picked her up in his arms and swung her around. "I was so proud of you!"

"How did you manage to make an airline lose my luggage?"

He soberered. "That, I didn't do."

She narrowed her gaze on him. "But if you could have...?"

He grinned.

"And how did you get here before me?"

"A few people owed me a few favors. We were in the same airport at the same time in San Francisco, you know. I simply managed to get a flight out first, on a different airline with a different destination and got here a good six hours before you. From that point on, it was easy."

He set her on her feet. "How does this strike you as a honeymoon suite?"

"Honeymoon?"

"I mean, just until we can get a flight out to the Galápagos Islands. That's where I intend us to have our real honeymoon."

Ali drew in a deep breath. "Keith, we're not married. We can't have a honeymoon."

"Sure we can," he said. "We can break with tradition. We can work outside the normal routine. You're not as staid as you think you are, my Ali the Hun, throwing dishes, blushing like a cherry when my tablecloth fell off and kissing me until I thought my skin would boil. From the moment I met you, with your many contrasts, your crazy contradictions, your gutsiness and your timidity, your prim librarian bun and your crazy, flyaway hair, I was lost. With your eyes that looked so cool and serene, yet simmered with passion you didn't seem to know was in you, you slayed me."

"It was passion I didn't know I had until you unleashed it."

He drew her close, opened her robe, opened his and pressed their bodies together. "Honey, I haven't even begun to unleash it," he said.

With a laugh, Ali wiggled closer. "Oh, no?" she said. "Then what's this? A banana?"

LOVE & LAUGHTER™

MOTHER KNOWS BEST— MAYBE!

These matchmaking moms have had enough of their happy-to-be-single kids. How is a respectable woman to become a grandmother unless her offspring cooperates? There's nothing to be done except to get the kids down the aisle, even if they go kicking and screaming all the way!

Plans are made, schemes hatched, plots unraveled. Let the love and laughter begin!

Enjoy Matchmaking Moms (from hell) with:

#27 PILLOW TALK
by Kristine Rolofson

Available this September 1997
wherever Harlequin books are sold.

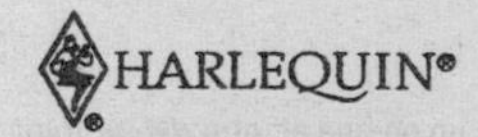

Look us up on-line at: http://www.romance.net MM997

LOVE & LAUGHTER LET'S CELEBRATE SWEEPSTAKES OFFICIAL RULES—NO PURCHASE NECESSARY

To enter, complete an Official Entry Form or 3" x 5" card by hand printing the words "Love & Laughter Let's Celebrate Sweepstakes," your name and address thereon and mailing it to: in the U.S., Love & Laughter Let's Celebrate Sweepstakes, P.O. Box 9076, Buffalo, NY 14269-9076, or in Canada to, Love & Laughter Let's Celebrate Sweepstakes, P.O. Box 637, Fort Erie, Ontario L2A 5X3. Limit: one entry per envelope, one prize to an individual, family or organization. Entries must be sent via first-class mail and be received no later than 11/30/97. No liability is assumed for lost, late, misdirected or nondelivered mail.

Three (3) winners will be selected in a random drawing (to be conducted no later than 12/31/97) from among all eligible entries received by D. L. Blair, Inc., an independent judging organization whose decisions are final, to each receive a collection of 15 Love & Laughter Romantic Comedy videos (approximate retail value: $250 U.S. per collection).

Sweepstakes offer is open only to residents of the U.S. (except Puerto Rico) and Canada who are 18 years of age or older, except employees and immediate family members of Harelquin Enterprises, Ltd., their affiliates, subsidiaries, and all other agencies, entities and persons connected with the use, marketing or conduct of this sweepstakes. All applicable laws and regulations apply. Offer void wherever prohibited by law. Taxes and/or duties on prizes are the sole responsibility of the winners. Any litigation within the province of Quebec respecting the conduct and awarding of prize may be submitted to the Régie des alcools, des courses et des jeux. All prizes will be awarded; winners will be notified by mail. No substitution for prizes is permitted. Odds of winning are dependent upon the number of eligible entries received.

Any prize or prize notification returned as undeliverable may result in the awarding of that prize to an alternative winner. By acceptance of their prize, winners consent to use of their names, photographs or likenesses for purposes of advertising, trade and promotion on behalf of Harlequin Enterprises, Ltd., without further compensation unless prohibited by law. In order to win a prize, residents of Canada will be required to correctly answer a time-limited, arithmetical skill-testing question administered by mail.

For a list of winners (available after December 31, 1997), send a separate stamped, self-addressed envelope to: Love & Laughter Let's Celebrate Sweepstakes Winner, P.O. Box 4200, Blair, NE 68009-4200, U.S.A.

LLRULES